When his lips ⟨…⟩ **she almost g**⟨…⟩ **reaction.**

She was reaching the point of no return, but she was also afraid to go along with the delicious desires that were sweeping over her. With an effort, she pulled herself away.

She looked up into Nick's eyes and saw only tenderness.

'I'm sorry,' she whispered. 'It's been so long since…'

'Demelza!' Ianni was rushing towards her, his arms outstretched.

She knelt down and hugged the boy. Looking up, she saw that Nick was smiling. For an instant she allowed herself the luxury of imagining what it would be like if she were Ianni's mother and Nick was…

As a full-time writer, mother and grandmother, **Margaret Barker** says: 'I feel blessed with my lifestyle, which has evolved over the years and included working as a State Registered Nurse. My husband and I live in a sixteenth-century thatched house near the East Anglian Coast. We are still very much in love, which helps when I am describing the romantic feelings of my heroines. In fact, if I find the creative flow diminishing, my husband will often suggest we put in some more research into the romantic aspects that are eluding me at the time!'

Recent titles by the same author:

A CHRISTMAS TO REMEMBER
THE PREGNANT DOCTOR
RELUCTANT PARTNERS

THE GREEK SURGEON

BY

MARGARET BARKER

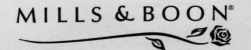

*First published in Great Britain 2002
Harlequin Mills & Boon Limited,
Eton House, 18-24 Paradise Road, Richmond, Surrey TW9 1SR*

© Margaret Barker 2002

ISBN 0 263 83060 8

*Set in Times Roman 10½ on 12 pt.
03-0402-48120*

*Printed and bound in Spain
by Litografía Rosés, S.A., Barcelona*

CHAPTER ONE

DEMELZA looked down over the stone wall bordering the terrace to find out what all the commotion was about. In the courtyard of the apartment below her she could see two small boys chasing each other round and round, laughing and calling to each other in Greek. Their skin was bronzed by the sun, one of them darker than the other. The lighter-skinned boy glanced up at her and she caught a glimpse of strong white teeth in a happy little face.

She felt a sudden pang of sadness. The boy looked about six years old, the same age as her own son would have been. Tears pricked behind her eyes, threatening to run down her cheeks. Well-meaning friends had told her that time would heal but the years had gone by and she was still hurting inside. She took a deep breath, brushed the moistness from her eyes and smiled down at the little boy.

He paused for a moment, looking up at her, before his playmate gave him a playful push and they continued their game. As she watched them she tried to imagine what it must be like to be so happy and carefree that you had to let off steam like that. They were both wearing the uniform of the nearby school, but from the rumpled state of their shirts it was obvious they'd had a hectic day.

The church clock above her on the hillside chimed six. The sun was dipping low in the sky behind her. It was still early in May but the afternoon had been very hot and she was looking forward to the comparative cool of the evening. Looking down at the two delightful little boys, she began to wonder who they belonged to.

They probably lived in the apartment below hers, but when she'd arrived from the airport this afternoon the place had seemed deserted. The door to the enclosed courtyard was now wide open, she noticed, and she distinctly remembered that she'd closed it. She'd felt suddenly nervous to be moving into this large old Greek villa, knowing no one, hundreds of miles from familiar territory.

There was the sound of footsteps on the old cobblestones outside the courtyard and a small, plump woman burst in, wiping her hands on her apron and beginning a tirade in Greek, directed towards the boys. It was obvious to Demelza that these two happy lads weren't supposed to be there. The woman was pointing towards the open gateway at the same moment as a tall man appeared.

He was carrying a black leather bag, which he put down on the flagstoned floor as he began to talk rapidly in Greek to the woman. She smiled, seemingly reassured as she dropped her agitated hands to her side. The boy who'd smiled up at Demelza ran with a whoop of joy towards the man and began chattering excitedly, his little arms fixed, limpet-like, around the man's waist. The woman put out her hand towards the other boy and led him away.

As the sturdy iron door of the courtyard clanged to behind the woman and her child, the tall man stopped speaking in Greek.

'Ianni, how many times have I told you that you

mustn't play here without telling Katerina where you are?'

Demelza was amazed by his flawless English. His suntanned olive skin, the handsome, rugged Mediterranean features, proclaimed him to be Greek, but his English accent was perfect. He was carrying the jacket of his grey suit over his arm, his open-necked white shirt almost as crumpled as the boy's. He looked tired, one hand now running through dark, tousled hair as he straightened up from speaking to the boy.

The little boy had assumed a contrite expression as he gazed up at the tall man. 'I'm sorry, Dad. Lefteris and I didn't mean to come in, but we were playing in the street outside his house and we just sort of found ourselves at this end. I only wanted to see if you were home.'

Perfect English again. Demelza was beginning to wonder who this bilingual father and son were as, for the first time since he'd arrived, the man looked up and noticed her. The sun, dipping down behind the hills, was in his eyes and he screwed up his eyes.

'Hello, you must be the new sister at the resort clinic. They told me you were coming today. I'm Nick Capodistrias.'

She remembered his name from the instructions the travel consortium who employed her had supplied. So this was Nicholas Capodistrias, the doctor she was to contact if there was something she couldn't handle in her new position.

She leaned further over the wall of her large flag-stoned terrace. 'I'm Demelza Tregarron. It's a relief to find we're going to be neighbours. I'll know where to get in touch with you if—'

She broke off, feeling that she was assuming an awful lot. Maybe Dr Capodistrias would think it an imposition if she asked for too much help, especially in his off-duty time. She'd been told he worked at the local hospital and he looked as if he'd welcome a bit of peace and quiet.

'I've been asked to look after you until you find your feet,' he said, his voice steady, giving nothing away as to how he felt about the arrangement. 'Why don't you come down and have a drink with us? We can't talk like this with you up there and the sun in my eyes.'

Young Ianni was jumping up and down excitedly now. 'Dad, can I have some lemonade?'

'Sure!' Dr Capodistrias turned to look up at Demelza. 'Are you coming?'

She was intensely aware that she hadn't finished unpacking and her belongings were strewn everywhere in her apartment, but she also knew that the sooner she began learning the ropes the easier life would become. And there was something intensely intriguing about this father and son. Was the little boy's mother inside, preparing supper and pouring drinks? If she was, why hadn't she come out to greet her husband?

There was so much to find out besides the useful information she needed to run the clinic. For the first time in six years she felt a spark of enthusiasm running through her. Taking the plunge and leaving the old life behind had been a good idea. At the ripe old age of thirty-two, she'd been in danger of stagnating.

'I'll be down in five minutes,' Demelza called, as she dashed inside her apartment to find something suitable to wear.

She couldn't go down in the skimpy shorts and sleeveless top she'd thrown on after her shower. First impressions were important and she didn't want Dr

Capodistrias to think she wasn't suitable to take charge of the new clinic at the beach resort. She mustn't look as if she was just another tourist out for a free holiday funded by a bit of work thrown in on the side.

She surveyed the chaos. The new white cotton trousers would go with her old tried-and-tested lime-green T-shirt. She wanted to look neat, informal, like an off-duty professional. A professional again! It had been a long time since she'd been in paid work and she wanted to give it her best shot.

Fully dressed, she glanced at herself in the long mirror as she ran a brush through her long auburn hair. She usually wore it coiled up on top of her head during the day, but in the evenings it felt so relaxing to have it tumbling casually over her shoulders.

She nudged herself along. Come on, girl, it's only a drink you're going for! As Demelza hurried down the outside stone staircase that led from her apartment to the courtyard, she noticed that whoever had converted this rather grand old villa into two apartments had done a good job. They'd kept the ancient ambience of the place whilst putting in all the mod cons that made life comfortable.

The plumbing left something to be desired but she'd been warned this wasn't a strong point in the Greek islands! But at least the shower had worked, even if she'd had to hold the shower head with one hand while she'd soaped herself with the other. Maybe she could persuade someone to attach it to the wall? Or perhaps she could do it herself. She'd been pretty nifty at DIY when she'd been running the domestic side of the farm.

She crossed the flagstoned courtyard and waited in front of the open door through which she'd seen the doctor and his son go into their apartment.

'Come through!' she heard Dr Capodistrias call from somewhere beyond the open door. 'We're out at the back.'

The interior of the apartment seemed dim after the bright sunlight. Demelza stepped straight into a large, rather grand living room, furnished with antique chairs, a table and a glass-fronted cupboard displaying delicate porcelain cups and saucers, antique silver ornaments and a large amount of cut glassware. Numerous portraits of family figures and groups adorned the walls.

She smiled as she noticed a bunch of spring flowers in pride of place in the middle of the table. It had been stuffed untidily inside a jam jar, obviously by Ianni's small hands, and it seemed charmingly incongruous with the rest of the decor.

She looked around her at the deserted room. There was no sign of his mother.

Nicholas Capodistrias suddenly appeared in the doorway that led to the outside terrace and extended his hand.

'Welcome!' he said impassively, as he shook her hand.

Demelza felt a strong hand enclosing her own and didn't pull away. It was good to have some physical contact with a fellow human being. She was startled by the warm feeling it gave her as she stood looking up into his dark brown eyes.

'Come and sit down.'

Young Ianni was already sitting at a small, rough-hewn wooden table, happily ploughing his way through a dish of crisps. He looked up at Demelza and tried to smile, but it was obviously difficult with his mouth full and the little boy gave an involuntary splutter of acknowledgement instead.

'Hey, save some for us!' his father said good-naturedly, moving the dish towards the centre of the table. 'What can I get you to drink?'

'Whatever you're having, Dr Capodistrias,' she replied politely.

'Call me Nick. And may I call you by your fascinating name? I've never met anyone called Demelza before.'

'It's Cornish. I was born in Cornwall and I was called after my grandmother.'

He was studying her with his expressive eyes. 'It's a lovely name. Now, you've asked for the same drink as me. I'm drinking ouzo, Demelza. Have you ever had any?'

She shook her head. 'I'd like to try some.'

He smiled, and she noticed how much younger and more approachable he looked with a smile on his face. He couldn't be older than his late thirties but the careworn expression he'd carried on his face when he'd first arrived home had given her the impression of an older man.

She noticed that the trousers of his grey suit had been replaced by a pair of old, worn jeans which outlined the strong muscles in his thighs. There was no doubt that he was a strikingly handsome man. A man who could speak fluent English and Greek, working out here on a sun-kissed island, in charge of a small, bewitching little son who'd already stolen her heart. The situation was intriguing her. She knew very little so far about him, but she found herself avid to find out more.

He was still smiling, but now with a hint of mischief. 'I feel I ought to warn you, ouzo's an acquired taste and it's very strong. I'll give you a small one and mix it with water.'

She watched as the clear liquid turned cloudy with the addition of the water. Raising the glass to her lips, she took a tentative sip. The liquid hit the back of her throat and made her gasp.

Father and son burst out laughing at her reaction.

'I did warn you!' Nick said.

Ianni had jumped to his feet and come round to her chair, patting her gently on the back with a small, soothing hand.

'Would you like some of my lemonade, Demella?'

She smiled at Ianni's mispronunciation of her name. What a perfectly charming boy! Demelza swallowed hard as she turned to look at the concerned little face so close to her own, peering over her shoulder.

'Lemonade would be lovely, Ianni. Thank you very much.'

The boy hurried away into the house to return with a large bottle. Solemnly he unscrewed the cap and was about to pour it into her ouzo glass.

Nick reached for a fresh glass and carefully supervised the pouring of the lemonade.

'See if you like it, Demella,' Ianni said anxiously.

She took a sip and gave it her serious consideration. 'It's excellent.'

Ianni smiled happily and settled back in his chair.

'Try Demelza's name again, Ianni,' Nick said. 'It starts off with Demel.'

'Demel…' Ianni said, carefully.

'Then finishes with za.'

'Za. Demelza, Demelza,' the little boy sang. 'Show me how to write it. I'll get my copy book.'

'Talking of which, did you do your homework at Katerina's?' Nick asked.

Ianni grinned. 'Most of it. I've only got to copy out some letters and then it's finished. Look, Demelza!'

She was amazed by the neatness of the little boy's exercise book and also by the fact that he was doing homework at such a tender age.

'Ianni is learning to read and write Greek and English at the same time, but he doesn't seem to have a problem with the work,' his father explained. 'Do you want to go and finish your homework inside the house so we don't disturb you with our chatter, Ianni?'

Ianni smiled. 'OK! I won't be long. And then can we go to Giorgio's for supper?'

'Didn't you have supper at Katerina's?'

Ianni pulled a face. 'I didn't eat much because I like having supper with you, Dad.' He glanced at Demelza. 'Why don't you come with us, Demelza? You'd like Giorgio's. Do you like dancing?'

Nick put a hand gently on his son's shoulder. 'Finish your homework and we'll see,' he said quickly.

As the little boy disappeared inside, Demelza turned to Nick. 'I really ought to get myself sorted out this evening.'

It was the talk of dancing that had alarmed her. She wasn't ready yet to throw herself into the social scene. One step at a time. She'd got herself out here and she didn't want to rush into things. Besides, she was sure that Nick wouldn't want an extra person intruding on his family supper. Especially someone who'd been dumped on him as an extra responsibility.

As if reading her thoughts, he leaned across the table towards her. 'If it's the dancing you're afraid of, don't worry—nobody has to join in unless they want to and it's only at the weekends that I let Ianni stay up for it. Tonight being Monday, I'll have him whisked away and in bed early enough to get a good night's sleep before school. So, if you'd like to taste the local cuisine, you'd be most welcome to join us. I don't expect you've got any food in the apartment.'

His voice was polite. She knew he was being the dutiful professional but she was loath to leave this warm family atmosphere to return to her lonely apartment.

'It's a very tempting idea,' she said carefully. 'And I do have a lot of questions to ask you about the clinic.'

'I'll fill you in and then you can ask me about anything you don't understand. When you start work in the morning you'll soon get the hang of the place. Basically...'

She listened attentively while Nick explained that she would be expected to do a morning surgery at the clinic on five days each week at the beach resort half a mile away. If there was anything she couldn't handle, she was to contact him at the hospital in the town. In between surgeries and at weekends, if there were any emergencies, the staff at the resort reception would contact her on her mobile and Demelza would decide if it was a case she could handle or if a visit to the hospital was required.

'You're not going to be rushed off your feet, Demelza. This is a new venture, which was deemed necessary because of the expanding number of tourists. Basically, you're the intermediary between the resort and the hospital.'

He paused. 'One thing puzzles me. Having read your qualifications and the fact that you were Sister of a busy surgical ward in London for a couple of years, I was wondering why you'd want to take such a relatively undemanding job?'

She raised her eyes to his but his enigmatic expression gave nothing away. 'My post in London was nearly seven years ago. I left it when I got married. Since then I've been running the domestic side of my husband's family farm.'

His dark eyes searched her face enquiringly. 'I didn't know that you'd had such a long gap in your career, but I'm sure the interview panel in London was satisfied with your curriculum vitae otherwise you wouldn't have been appointed.'

Demelza bristled at the cool tone of his voice. 'Don't worry, I'll be well able to cope with this job. My nursing training, my years as a staff nurse and my two years as a sister have equipped me to cope with any medical emergency. And my contract is only for six months, so if at the end of that time it isn't renewed then—'

'We'll see how things work out, Demelza,' he intervened. 'I wasn't questioning your ability to do the job. You may decide you want to take up a more demanding post in the UK, in which case you wouldn't want to renew your contract.'

He was staring intently at her as he cleared his throat. 'What does your husband think of all this?'

She felt the familiar churning of emotions whenever anyone referred to Simon. 'I'm a widow,' she said quietly.

An expression of deep compassion crossed his face. 'I'm sorry. Nobody told me. Yes, I can see why you might want to make a fresh start.' He paused and his voice became gentler. 'How long have you been widowed?'

'Six years.'

Nick looked surprised. 'And you haven't thought of going back to work before now?'

'It wasn't as simple as that. I've often wanted to but it wasn't possible.'

'And now it is?'

'Yes. You see, my husband's brother has recently married a very capable girl and I felt she could safely take over my duties, so I seized my chance.'

It all sounded so easy when she put it like that, but she wasn't going to fill him in on any of the details, not yet anyway. Not until she knew him better. First she'd lost her husband, then her son, followed by the long years when she'd often felt like a prisoner at the farm, having to cope with her own emotional suffering and that of Simon's parents, who'd clung to her as if she were their real daughter.

Then she'd had to see if the new daughter-in-law had been willing to replace her and had the necessary skills to cope with what had become a very demanding job, both physically and emotionally. Only when she'd been absolutely sure that Jane could fill her shoes had she planned her escape.

She raised her eyes and saw that Nick was still watching her with a puzzled expression.

'You look like a woman who's suffered,' he said quietly, his hand reaching across the table to cover her own.

The touch of his fingers unnerved her. A woman could lose herself looking into this charismatic man's eyes, those dark brown pools of compassion. He would be an excellent doctor. She wouldn't mind being his patient if he put on that expression when he cared for her. It was a poignant moment for her. Another step towards joining the human race again.

Ianni came dashing outside, holding his copy book for Demelza to read. She looked at the beautifully formed characters, one page in Greek and one page in English.

'It's very good, Ianni.'

The little boy smiled. 'So, are we all going to Giorgio's, Dad?'

Nick looked at Demelza enquiringly.

She smiled. 'I'd like that very much.'

Ianni put his small hand in hers and began to tug her away from the table. 'Come on, then!'

Giorgio's taverna exuded warmth and hospitality. Giorgio himself, a gnarled, weather-beaten character of indeterminate age, definitely on the wrong side of fifty but with the mischievous grin of a twenty-year-old, was playing an accordion and singing a lively song in Greek. His eyes lit up as they walked in and he nodded his head towards Nick before quickly finishing the song, putting down his accordion and hurrying over to greet the newcomers.

'Nico!' Giorgio greeted the younger man with an enthusiastic hug, before reaching down to hoist little Ianni onto his shoulder, chattering to the young boy in rapid Greek.

Ianni laughed at what was said to him and replied in a rapid torrent that had the taverna owner laughing along with him. Demelza felt sure that whatever was under discussion had something to do with her. She hung back, reluctant to break up the warm ambience of the group, but Giorgio, still with the boy on his shoulder, held out his hand and grasped hers.

'Welcome,' he said enthusiastically. 'What will you have to drink? Any friend of Nico is already a friend of mine. Drinks on the house! Ouzo? Retsina…?'

'Lemonade, please,' Demelza said quickly, as they

were shown to a table on a large, vine-covered terrace overlooking the bay.

Giorgio raised one dark, bushy eyebrow at her request. 'Lemonade is for the children. I will bring you a bottle of beautiful wine. They make it across the water in Crete. You will like it, Demelza.'

'And a bottle of water to go with it, please, Giorgio,' Nick said quickly.

He was smiling contentedly as he settled himself against the back of his ancient iron seat, looking at Demelza across the table. Ianni had pulled his chair close to hers. Giorgio had already returned to his accordion and was singing again whilst a couple of charming young waiters were setting out wine, glasses and a basket of bread on the table.

She found herself relaxing as she hadn't done for years. Looking out beyond the terrace, she saw the sun dipping down behind the mountains across the bay, casting variegated shadows over the water. The sun was a fiery red as it disappeared and the sky glowed with a diffusion of pinks and orange.

'Come and choose what you would like to eat.' Nick stood up and led Demelza over towards the interior of the taverna.

The kitchen was chaotic. A middle-aged woman—Giorgio's wife, presumably—was standing beside a huge cooking range, stirring something in a large pan. She lifted one hand to wave across at Nick and Demelza before continuing her stirring, smiling at them as they surveyed the vast array of dishes set out for their inspection. Nick explained what each dish contained as he gave Demelza a guided tour of what was on offer.

Lamb stew, moussaka, various kinds of chicken, aubergine, beef stiffado, which was a kind of savoury casserole, fish, lobster, prawns… She found it difficult to decide. It had been a long day since she'd checked in at Gatwick Airport and all the new experiences were beginning to overwhelm her.

'Would you like me to choose?' Nick asked quietly.

She nodded gratefully. 'Something small for me. Perhaps—'

'I'll get something we can share,' he told her.

When the food arrived at the table, Demelza found she could pick and choose from the plates of mezze, different succulent Greek dishes set out in an appetising way. The small helpings of aubergine, stuffed vine leaves called dolmades, prawns, grilled fish and chicken stimulated her appetite and tasted delicious washed down with the Cretan wine.

'I hadn't realised I was so hungry,' she said, as she put down her fork and leaned back against her chair.

The sky was now dark, but lit up by a crescent moon. Behind the taverna, she could just make out the outline of the mysterious hills, waiting to be explored whenever she was able to find the time in her new life. She was sure she could detect the smell of the oregano which she'd noticed on the hillside above her apartment. It was an idyllic setting in which to live and work.

Ianni, pulling his chair even closer to hers, had laid his head on her lap and closed his eyes. Automatically, she reached for the small boy and pulled him onto her lap, where he fell into a deep sleep.

Demelza looked across the table at Nick who was watching her, a strange expression on his face.

'Here, let me take him,' he said quietly. 'Ianni can become a bit of a weight when he's dead to the world.'

She shook her head. 'I don't mind,' she said softly.

That was an understatement if ever there was one! She was revelling in the feeling of this small, sleeping child on her lap.

The noise of plates clattering onto tables, people laughing and joking, Giorgio playing his accordion and singing loudly didn't disturb young Ianni.

'I'd better take Ianni to bed soon,' Nick said. 'I usually have him settled by now.' He continued to watch her across the table. 'You look as if you're used to children.'

She realised that Nick was trying discreetly to find out if she had any of her own. Everyone always did. Sooner or later the dreaded question would surface and she would have to steel herself to make a reply.

'I love children,' she said slowly. 'I was expecting a little boy, six years ago, but I miscarried when I was six months pregnant.'

She swallowed hard, breathing deeply as she'd learned to do—anything to prevent herself from crying. She should have got over it by now. Other people did but for some reason the dreams of what might have been wouldn't go away. If Simon hadn't died before she'd lost the baby they would have had another child and her miscarriage would be a distant memory.

'I'm sorry. That must have been awful for you.'

Nick's voice was sympathetic and sincere. She raised her eyes from the sleeping child and looked at him. She felt she could trust him.

'Sometimes I feel as if I'll never get over it.'

He reached across the table and took her hand in his. 'You'll never forget, but you will get over it in time. Grief doesn't last for ever even though it seems as if it will.'

'Yes, but six years!'

She bit her lip. Why was she confiding in this relative stranger? She'd said more to him than she'd admitted to anyone for a long time.

'If you'd been able to have another child, that would have eased some of the grief in your heart,' he said, his voice husky with emotion.

She gazed into the dark, expressive eyes. Here was a man who was used to counselling his patients in their unhappiness. He'd understood her feelings exactly. It was good to find someone she could really trust. For so long she'd kept her feelings bottled up, trying to appear strong and brave for the rest of Simon's family.

'I was surrounded by Simon's family, but there were times when I felt I was totally alone in my grief,' she said quietly. 'I felt there was no one who understood what I was going through.'

Nick nodded his head sympathetically. 'It's a terrible thing to lose your partner in life.'

She swallowed hard. From his understanding tone, she began to wonder if Ianni's mother was dead.

'Are you…bringing up Ianni by yourself?' Demelza asked carefully.

Nick's eyes flickered but his expression didn't change. 'Ianni's mother lives in England.'

'Does Ianni spend time with her?'

'Sometimes, but Lydia leads a very busy life and finds it difficult to fit Ianni into her complicated schedule. Actually, she's coming out for a holiday some time this year.'

'That will be nice.'

Nick raised an eyebrow. 'Nice for Ianni, I hope. Lydia will be staying at the beach resort, of course. I couldn't cope with having her at the apartment. We're divorced.'

Demelza felt a sudden change taking place in her emotions. She had no designs on this charming, sympathetic doctor whatsoever—indeed, on any man who might cross her path—but the fact that he was relatively free made him certainly more interesting.

Nick stood up and came round to her chair, reaching down to take his sleeping son into his arms. She felt the brush of his strong hands against her as she released the small boy. It was a warm, comforting feeling, this contact with a compassionate man. He hadn't told her to snap out of it, to pull herself together, to get on with her life. But for the first time in years that was exactly what she felt she should do.

CHAPTER TWO

DEMELZA found the clinic better equipped than she'd expected. Everything was brand new. The travel consortium had spared no expense and Nick had told her the previous evening that if there was anything she found she needed she was to put in a request.

'We're hoping for super-efficient medical facilities down there at the beach resort,' he'd said, just before he'd gone into his apartment, carrying his sleeping son.

They'd talked in hushed whispers as they'd hurried along the narrow street from the village back to the old villa. The conversation had been completely professional. It had almost been as if both of them had felt they'd been too familiar during this first evening together, but on leaving the warm atmosphere of the taverna they'd become purely professional colleagues.

Climbing the stone stairs to her apartment, Demelza had wished the warm rapport had been maintained to the end of their evening together. But perhaps it had been a good idea to get back on a professional footing. It had been obvious that Nick was totally wrapped up in his medical work and caring for his son and she...well, she wasn't ready for anything other than a friendly relationship with anyone.

Least of all with a handsome Greek doctor, she thought as she looked out of her surgery window across the smooth sweep of the sandy beach and the dazzling blue of the Mediterranean. Children were already playing out on the sand; adults, semi-clad in bright, garish, sometimes fluorescent holiday clothes, were trooping down to spread their towels on the sunbeds nearest the sea.

She wouldn't mind an hour or two in the sun herself to try and put some colour in her pale skin. Perhaps at the end of the morning, if there were no demands on her time, she could have a picnic lunch out there. She looked at the computer on her desk; it was all very high tech for a Greek island. She'd been warned about power cuts, so she would make sure she saved all vital information onto floppy disks.

There was no patient list to tell her who was coming in this morning. Tourists simply turned up and waited their turn. She could hear a murmur of voices in the waiting room outside and pressed the bell that told the first one to come in.

'Bryony Driver.' A tall, thin woman of about forty announced herself as she came in. 'I had to come and see you, Sister, because I feel absolutely lousy. In the middle of the night I felt terrible. Yesterday I was OK but today…ugh!'

Demelza pulled her chair closer to Bryony's. She preferred to sit on the patient's side of her desk. It helped to break the ice and remove any barriers the patient might feel.

'Have you felt as bad as this before, Bryony?'

'Oh, yes! My doctor says I've got some kind of depression. He gave me some pills, which seemed to help, but I don't want to be relying on pills for the rest of my life. So I thought if I went on holiday I could try and manage without them. I mean, it's so lovely out here, I feel I ought to be able to pull myself together and shake off my depression without needing pills.'

'What pills are you on, Bryony?' Demelza asked carefully.

Bryony shrugged. 'Some kind of tranquillisers. My doctor at home keeps changing them.'

Bryony was fishing about in her large shoulder-bag, placing lipsticks, a comb, a cheque book and purse on the corner of Demelza's desk.

'Here they are!' Bryony brought out the box of pills with a triumphant flourish. 'I thought doing nothing in the sun all day would cheer me up. I was planning to flush them down the loo just to show I could...'

The air of bravado disappeared completely. Bryony's face crumpled and she began to sob. 'I just can't forget him.'

'Who can't you forget?' Demelza asked gently.

'That two-timing husband of mine! Oh, he's given me plenty of money and the house so I can't grumble about that, but I just can't forget that he's with some-body else.'

Demelza nodded sympathetically. 'I see. How long are you staying out here, Bryony?'

Bryony shrugged. 'All summer if I want to. I've got nothing to go back to England for. They've told me I can have my room in the resort for as long as I want it.'

Demelza glanced at the box of tablets, making a note of the name. One of the newer brand of tranquillisers which had been well received in the medical press and had no known side effects. Throughout the years when she'd been confined to the farm, she'd made a point of keeping up with the medical trends in her reading, hop-ing that one day she would be able to return to the profession she loved. This had enabled her to answer

all the questions the interview panel in London had put
to her about contemporary medicine.

'I think you should go back on your pills, Bryony,'
she told her patient. 'Take them for a week and then
come back and see me again. If you're worried, don't
hesitate to come before then.'

Bryony's face relaxed and she smiled. 'It's good to
talk, isn't it? Sometimes that's all it takes, a shoulder
to cry on. I didn't sleep all night, never do. I've got
some sleeping pills with me, but I'm trying not to get
hooked on them.'

'Well, don't take the sleeping pills while you're on
your other pills,' Demelza said quickly. 'You mustn't
mix your tablets. Stick to the tranquillisers and if
you're awake in the night, read a light book or glance
through a magazine. You can snooze on the beach if
you get sleepy during the day. Just try to relax and take
things easy.'

Bryony stood up. 'Thanks ever so much. What's
your name?'

'Demelza.'

'What a lovely name! Sister Demelza. Has a nice
ring to it, doesn't it? Do you know, Sister, you're the
first friend I've made here at the resort. I'll look forward to seeing you again next week.'

Demelza smiled. 'Take care of yourself, Bryony.'

As the door closed behind her patient she was thinking, Poor woman! Which was more painful—to be widowed or for your husband to leave you for someone
else?

She pressed the bell for the next patient.

There was a steady stream of minor complaints
throughout the morning, including a couple of patients
with upset stomachs. They seemed to be improving al-

ready and she didn't envisage an epidemic. That was one thing that she must check on in a resort of this size where tourists were living side by side. One of the things she told her patients was the importance of drinking only bottled water.

One patient had a hacking cough which had kept him and his wife awake in the night. Fortunately, he'd brought his prescribed medication with him from England and merely needed some reassurance from Demelza after she'd given his chest a full examination. It was only the second day of his holiday and Demelza assured him that the sun and the relaxation should speed his recovery. If there was no improvement in a few days, she suggested he should come back and see her again.

There was a mild case of sunburn from a fair-skinned patient but it looked as if this had been caught in time. She'd told the patient to stay out of the sun and given her a soothing cream to apply at intervals. Looking out of the window as the midday sun beat down on the beach, she could see a few potential patients for tomorrow! When would they ever learn to take it easy and apply high-factor sun creams or, better still, stay under the sun umbrellas for long periods?

She finished her notes for the morning and switched off the computer. Everything seemed quiet in the waiting room. Irini, the helpful young Greek nurse who doubled up as receptionist, had already gone off duty now that there were no more patients.

Demelza went across to the fridge and took out the food she'd prepared that morning. She'd bought a couple of bread rolls from the village bakery and a few slices of salami from the shop she'd passed on her way to the beach. She could change out of the white uniform dress supplied by the company into her shorts and sun top before finding herself a sunbed and umbrella near the edge of the water.

Glancing through the surgery window, she could already imagine the feel of the warmth on her sun-starved legs. Mmm...

She picked up the sports bag that held everything she would need for this relaxing afternoon and opened the door of the waiting room.

A woman in a sandy swimsuit was hurrying inside from the beach, carrying a small boy in her arms.

'Oh, thank goodness I've caught you, Sister! They told me the clinic would be shut by now. Harry was jumping off the rocks and he's hurt his arm.'

'You'd better come into the surgery.' Demelza ushered them through, all thoughts of the sun instantly forgotten. 'Now, Harry, will you let me have a look at your arm?'

The little boy continued to whimper as he sat on his mother's lap, staring with frightened eyes at Demelza.

'I'm not going to hurt you, Harry,' Demelza said reassuringly, as she placed her fingers gently on the boy's arm.

It was obvious to her, even without examination, that one or both of the bones in the lower arm were fractured. The unnatural angle at which the hand was now flexed was the deciding factor in her diagnosis. She decided not to put the little boy through any more stress until the arm could be manipulated and set in its correct position. An X-ray was essential to confirm her diagnosis and for that he would need to go to the hospital, but first she would make her little patient as comfortable as possible.

Gently, she explained what was happening to the

anxious mother, before fixing the injured arm onto a splint and into a sling. Picking up the phone, she dialled the hospital and asked to speak to Dr Nicholas Capodistrias.

Her spirits lifted at the sound of his deep, calm voice. 'Nick Capodistrias here.'

'Nick, it's Demelza. I've got a young patient with an injury to the lower right arm. From the angle of the hand, I suspect he's fractured the ulna.'

'The resort driver will drive you to the hospital. Will you bring him in, Demelza?'

Nick was professional to the point of abruptness. Demelza replied in the same tone and agreed to be at the hospital as soon as possible.

As soon as Harry's mother had thrown a dress on over her swimsuit they were on the narrow, winding road that led from the beach towards the town a couple of miles away. Stavros, the resort driver, drove as if he were a competitor in a rally. Demelza, sitting beside him, found herself hanging onto her seat whilst Stavros drove, one hand on the wheel, gently humming to himself a haunting Greek melody which she remembered hearing the night before in Giorgio's taverna.

Demelza glanced behind her to reassure herself that her patient wasn't coming to any harm as the resort people-carrier swayed from side to side. She was glad she'd put the arm in a sturdy splint. Little Harry's eyes were closed as he leaned against his mother, but he'd stopped whimpering.

The whole journey took only a few minutes but Demelza felt great relief as she stepped out and opened the back door for her patient and his mother.

It was a small, new hospital, not more than three or four years old. A nurse in Reception took them along to a small accident and emergency department. Demelza recognised Nick before he turned round from bending over a patient.

He moved towards her with that languid, athletic swing she'd come to admire. His white shirt was open at the neck in a casual manner, but the crisp grey trousers were still impeccably pressed. He looked every inch the successful, efficient doctor.

'So this is our new patient,' he said gently. 'What's your name?'

'Harry,' the little boy said. 'Are you going to make my arm better?'

'I'm going to try,' Nick said, carefully unwrapping the splint. 'First, I'm going to take a picture of your arm so that I can see what's wrong with it.'

'My mum thinks it's broken,' the little boy said.

'Nothing that can't be fixed,' Nick said reassuringly. 'I've been mending broken bones for years. How old are you, Harry?'

'I'm six, but I'm big for my age. Everybody thinks I'm seven.'

Nick smiled. 'Yes, I think you could pass for a seven-year-old. I've got a little boy who's six and I think he's a bit smaller than you.'

'What's his name?' Harry asked.

'Ianni,' Nick replied, gently stroking the boy's hair in a soothing gesture.

They were already in the radiology department with Harry on the table, waiting for the X-rays to be taken. Demelza was impressed by the calm way that Nick worked, keeping up a constant flow of conversation with his patient so that the little boy seemed to have lost his fear of the unfamiliar surroundings and the antiseptic smell that pervaded the hospital.

'He's a super doctor, isn't he?' Harry's mother whispered to Demelza as Nick busied himself with the X-ray. 'I wonder where he learned to speak such good English.'

'I don't know,' Demelza murmured, thinking that was one of the mysteries surrounding this man that she intended to solve.

The thought crossed her mind that it might have been pillow talk with his wife that had improved his English. She was surprised how she didn't like to think about that! She'd become fond of this helpful doctor in the few hours she'd known him and she liked to think of him as being completely unattached, apart from his delightful son, of course.

'You were right, Sister,' Nick said, coming across to show her the developed films. 'Transverse fracture of the ulna. Can you see it?'

She nodded as she studied the X-rays. 'Have you got a plaster technician on duty?'

Nick smiled down at her. 'We all have to turn our hands to everything in this hospital. I took the X-rays and I'll set the arm myself. Would you help me, please, Sister? We haven't any spare staff at the moment. At the end of the morning there's a general exodus for the long midday break. Unless there's an emergency, the hospital has only a skeleton staff in the afternoons. We've all got mobiles so there would be no problem to call back staff early if they were required.'

'Of course I'll help,' Demelza said quickly. 'Just show me where you keep the equipment and—'

'Through here. We do have a small plaster room, even if there's nobody in there at the moment.'

Harry was curled up on his mother's knee, watching Demelza as she soaked the bandages in preparation for application. Nick carefully lifted the little boy up onto the treatment table, carefully but expertly manipulating the bone into the correct position.

'You can pass me the first bandage now, Sister,' he said, quietly. 'Are you OK, Harry?'

The little boy nodded. 'When you've finished winding that stuff round my arm, will it be mended?'

Nick smiled. 'Well, it's not quite as quick as that, Harry. It's going to take about five weeks for the broken bones to mend. I expect you'll be back in England by then, won't you?'

'We go home at the end of next week, Doctor,' Harry's mother said.

'Can't we stay out here until my arm's better?' Harry asked brightly. 'It would be much better for my arm, wouldn't it, Doctor? I mean, that plane journey can't be good for broken arms, can it?'

Nick laughed. 'Good try, Harry! What does Mum think?'

Harry's mother thought that Dad needed to get back to work to earn some more money so they could come out again next year.

'And you'll have your nice new plaster to keep your arm safe on the plane, Harry,' Demelza put in. 'If you let me know your flight details I'll send a note to the airline and ask them to take extra special care of you.'

'And I'll give you a letter to give to your own doctor when you get home,' Nick said, putting the final touches to the plaster. 'There we go! You'll be as good as new in a few weeks, just so long as you don't start jumping off any more rocks. Promise me you won't do anything like that, Harry.'

Harry pulled a wry face. 'I promise…but I can play a bit, can't I?'

'Of course you can.'

Harry's mother was smiling as they walked with her to the outer door.

'Stavros will take you back to the beach resort,' Nick said.

He turned to look down at Demelza. 'You don't have to go back just yet, do you, Sister? I thought you might like to look round the hospital while you're here.'

She smiled. 'I'd like that very much. I've got a bag in the car with everything I need for the day so I'll just get it out before Stavros goes back to the resort.'

She went out to the car and helped to settle Harry and his mother in the back, smilingly requesting Stavros to take great care of her patient. Perhaps drive a little more slowly over the bumpy road down to the beach?

Stavros grinned back at Demelza. 'No problem, Sister,' he told her, letting in the clutch and hurtling off along the road, leaving a cloud of dust trailing behind him.

Nick was studying some case notes as he waited for her in Reception.

Demelza was shaking her head worriedly as she joined him. 'He's a fiendishly fast driver, our Stavros, isn't he? Where did you recruit him from? The Monte Carlo Rally?'

Nick smiled. 'Don't worry about Stavros. That's the way most of the young men out here drive and he can't drive any other way. We haven't lost a patient yet.'

'Well, that's reassuring.'

Nick was giving the notes back to the duty nurse. He turned round and put a hand under Demelza's elbow, guiding her gently towards the corridor.

'I thought we'd start with the wards—the medical

ward is just along here. Like all our departments, it's very small compared with the other hospitals you will have worked in.'

The touch of Nick's hand under her arm was pleasant as Demelza walked along the corridor. What a kind man he was, and so courteous. She was definitely beginning to feel that she wasn't a burden to him, that he wasn't regretting having had her foisted upon him.

'It's good of you to show me round,' she said politely as Nick pushed open the door to the ward. 'I mean, I suppose this is your lunch-hour.'

Nick grinned, his features taking on the appealing characteristics she'd noticed in his charming little son. 'You obviously haven't lived on a Greek island before. Everything grinds to a halt at midday and relaxation takes over. As I said before, unless there's an emergency, we have a long lunch and rest afterwards. Things get back to normal about five or six.'

There were only six beds in the medical ward, with a curtain dividing the male section from the female. Two men and a woman were sitting at a table at one end of the ward, having lunch. There was a bottle of wine on the table, and Demelza could see a large crusty loaf, some feta cheese and a dish of olives and tomatoes amongst the other appetising-looking dishes.

A nurse in a white cotton dress was just about to sit down at the table with her patients. She smiled at Nick and said something in rapid Greek.

Nick replied, before turning to explain to Demelza that the nurse was asking if they would like to have some lunch.

'I said we had to get on with our tour of the hospital.'

'The patients look so happy!' she remarked. 'What a great atmosphere you have in here!'

'They look forward to a glass of wine or two with their lunch. And unless they're really ill or on medication that contra-indicates wine, there's no reason why they shouldn't indulge themselves. The lady is recovering from pneumonia. Both the men have had cardiac problems which have been resolved and, as they keep on reminding me, a reasonable amount of red wine is supposed to be good for their arteries.'

Nick spent a few minutes chatting with the patients who were all obviously delighted to see him. Then it was on to inspect the surgical ward, which was of a similar size. Two male patients were sitting at the dining table while a nurse was helping a couple of bed-ridden patients.

Demelza was beginning to feel a warm glow about this tiny hospital. There was a lot of tender loving care going on in here. Even in the small operating theatre, she found a nurse lovingly polishing the handles on the cupboards.

'Shouldn't that nurse be having her lunch?' Demelza asked as she and Nick went out into the corridor.

'Eleni will go when she's satisfied that the theatre is perfect in every way. We don't have set hours here.'

'I'm very impressed with the hospital,' Demelza said. 'I'm beginning to see what life out here is really like.'

Nick paused in the corridor outside the small obstetric ward. 'Well, as you're so interested, if you'd like to spend the afternoon with me, I could also show you something of my island.'

She heard the pride in his voice as he'd said 'my island'.

'Your island?' she queried gently.

'I was born here,' he said proudly. 'Oh, I had to live in England for many years but I came back as soon as I could. There's no place on earth like Kopelos.'

There was a catch in his voice as he finished off his sentence. She wanted to ask so many questions about why he'd had to live in England, but it was early days and she didn't want to appear too inquisitive. Little by little, she hoped he would reveal the story of his life to her during the long hot summer she was to spend on this delightful island.

'I want to get to know this island very much,' she said. 'Thank you. I hadn't made any plans for this afternoon except to relax in the sun on the beach.'

'Ah, not the crowded beach at the resort!' Nick said. 'I'll take you to a quiet beach where you'll hear nothing but the sound of the sea, the bleating of the lambs on the hillside...' He broke off and smiled. 'We'd better get on with the tour before I get carried away. This is the obstetrics ward, as you can see...'

There were a couple of young mothers looking after their babies in the tiny ward. A nurse came over to talk to Nick in rapid Greek. He introduced Demelza and the conversation changed to English.

Demelza smiled at one of the young mothers who had finished feeding her baby and was proudly dressing her in a tiny white gown.

'What a beautiful baby!'

'Here, take!' the mother said, handing the baby over to Demelza.

As she snuggled the baby against her, Demelza noticed that indefinable smell all babies had when they'd just been powdered and pampered and put into clean clothes. A lump rose at the back of her throat as she looked at the dear little rosebud mouth, the tiny dimpled cheeks, the dark lashes like a curtain over the baby's precious eyes.

If she was to work with babies again she would have to steel herself and be totally professional. She couldn't allow the loss of her unborn son to colour her treatment of babies. Maybe it would get easier with time, but for the moment...

She forced herself to keep smiling as she handed back the baby. A lifetime of other people's babies spread ahead of her and she was going to have to cope with her emotions better than she was doing at present.

Back home on the farm she'd deliberately banished the dream of having babies of her own. It had been impossible to imagine being in another relationship. And babies should be born with two loving parents. Yes, she'd had a wonderful loving relationship but it was a beautiful experience from the past. She had to move on. It was early days, but she recognised that leaving the farm and starting a new life out here had been the best move she could have made.

She gave herself a mental shake as she concentrated all her attention on getting to know the hospital and how it worked. There was no doubt she would have to work closely with Nick and the hospital staff, and it was essential that she find out all she can.

'It's a great little hospital, Nick,' she said, as he escorted her out through the front door.

'It's very compact, but we can deal with most uncomplicated cases of medicine, surgery, obstetrics, gynaecology and orthopaedics. Obviously, the cases we can't handle are taken to hospitals in Athens or Rhodes.'

He was striding ahead of her along the small parking

area in front of the hospital. 'Here's my car, Demelza. As you can see, I parked it under the largest tree for the sake of the shade, but it's going to feel very hot until the air-conditioning kicks in.'

It was a sturdy-looking, four-wheel-drive vehicle. Nick unlocked the doors and Demelza climbed up into the front passenger seat. The hot leather felt scorching through her thin cotton dress. She put her bag by her feet.

'Will it be possible to change into my shorts when we get to this beach?' she asked.

Nick was turning on the air-conditioning. 'Of course. And we can have a swim to cool off.'

They headed away from the town on a narrow road carved out of the hillside.

'When I was a boy, this was a mere donkey track,' Nick said, changing down into a lower gear. 'We used to come up here to play sometimes. My mother would send me out to get fresh herbs and I'd take a couple of friends and we'd forget what time it was. Sometimes we even used to forget the herbs! That was when I was only about five or six. It was a big change when I went to live in England and found that children couldn't roam around freely like we do here.'

'Why did you go to live in England?'

Nick took a deep breath. 'Ah, that's a long story.'

Demelza glanced across, but Nick's eyes held a veiled expression. He was making it perfectly obvious that he didn't want to talk about it. There was a sadness in the way his shoulders had suddenly drooped. The air of devil-may-care was missing as he kept his eyes studiously on the narrow road ahead.

She leaned back against her seat and allowed the welcome cool air from the air-conditioning to revive her spirits. Beneath Nick's confident exterior there was a deep vulnerability about him. He obviously loved living on this island—who wouldn't? She was already in love with the place. So it must have been terrible for a young boy to be transplanted to England. She sensed there had been some sort of crisis in the family.

His handsome, dark features and Mediterranean mannerisms proclaimed him to be essentially Greek, but perhaps his mother had been English? She didn't want to pry. If she managed to gain his confidence he would perhaps fill her in on his background. She was intrigued by him, by the depth of his character and the secrets which seemed to be hidden beneath the surface. She found herself longing to know more about him and felt surprised by the way she was feeling. It was a long time since she'd been so curious about a man.

Since Simon's death she'd felt like a nun, having absolutely no interest in the opposite sex. But here she was, driving along beside a very handsome, drop-dead-gorgeous man and not feeling the least bit intimidated. Feeling, in fact, nothing but admiration and the desire to get to know him better.

'There's the bay we're going to!' Nick pointed ahead as they crested the hill.

She glanced sideways at him and caught the flash of strong white teeth in his dark, animated face. The car lurched from the metalled road onto a stony track and Demelza found herself hanging onto her seat. She was glad of the restraining seat belt as Nick carefully negotiated the potholes in the track.

'We had a lot of rain during the winter and it will be weeks before anyone gets around to attempting to mend this section of road. Very few people use it so it's not a priority on the island. I asked the mayor of

Kopelos town about it a few days ago and he simply
smiled, spread his hands in front of him and said,
''*Avrio!*''''

'Which means?'

Nick laughed. 'Tomorrow! You'll hear that word a
lot around here. The philosophy is that most things can
wait until tomorrow. It leads to a relaxed style of life
but some very bumpy roads.'

Demelza glanced out of her side window and felt a
shiver of fear at the sight of the sheer drop.

Nick took one hand off the steering-wheel and patted
her hand. 'Don't worry, Demelza. I've driven down
this track many times. You're quite safe.'

He removed his hand to steady the wheel. She was
surprised to find that she missed the touch of his fingers
but was relieved to see the intense concentration on his
face. Glancing sideways again out of her window, she
concentrated on the beauty of the ravine below her
rather than the danger of the road. Fir trees sprawled
up the sides of the hills and somewhere in the depths
of the valley she caught a glimpse of water, a precious
commodity on this island. It was only a small river,
she saw, making its way to the blue expanse of the
bay.

'Nearly there!' Nick said. 'That's the worst bit over.'

Demelza breathed a sigh of relief as the track even-
tually opened out into a wide, sandy swathe of land,
bordering the sea.

'We'll leave the car here and walk down to the
beach. It's too rocky to go any further. I'll get the food
out of the back. Do you want to change here? It's pretty
hot out there.'

Demelza nodded, feeling suddenly embarrassed
about undressing. She only had to pull her bikini on

under her uniform dress and then whip off the dress but...

'I'll take the stuff down to the beach and you can follow when you're ready,' Nick said, in a matter-of-fact voice.

Problem solved! She flashed him a grateful smile as she climbed down from her seat. The afternoon heat hit her. It was only May. What was it going to be like in the real summer months?

She stood behind the car and quickly changed into her new white bikini, noting that it was only slightly whiter than her own skin. Extricating the sunblock from her bag, she applied some to every inch of her bare skin. She wasn't going to take any chances. Besides which, she had a whole six months in which to acquire her safe tan.

Glancing around the side of the car, she saw that Nick had disappeared beyond the trees onto the beach. Picking up her bag, she hurriedly followed in the direction she'd seen him going. She felt a certain excitement rising up inside her. It was so amazing to be a long way from England on a deserted beach with a handsome stranger. She felt as if she'd shed ten years since arriving on this island. She was alive again after the arid, desert years.

She saw him immediately as she walked over the small dune at the edge of the beach. He was spreading a rug on the sand. She noticed that he'd already changed into black, figure-hugging swimming shorts and with a shock she recognised the frisson of excitement that ran through her. It wasn't desire exactly, or was it? If it wasn't desire, it was something dangerously similar.

He raised his head and waved his hand as he saw her coming. She took a deep breath to steady herself.

CHAPTER THREE

NICK stood up and came to meet Demelza as she hurried down the beach. He was reaching down to take her bag when he paused to give her a quizzical look.

'You're out of breath, Demelza. You should have taken your time. It's too hot to hurry in this heat.'

Her breathlessness had nothing to do with hurrying! She was experiencing the strangest feelings at the sight of Nick in those flatteringly macho swimming shorts. It was a long time since she'd seen a handsome man like Nick with so few clothes on and at such close quarters. It was having an unnerving effect on her which she could only describe as pleasant...well, actually, if she was truly honest, which she was trying not to be, it was more than pleasant!

She tried to banish the thoughts but they wouldn't go. She recognised that it was all part of her reawakening and she would have to deal with it very carefully.

'We'd better swim first before we have lunch. As we all know, it's not a good idea to swim on a full stomach,' Nick said, putting Demelza's bag on the sand beside the rug.

'I've only brought a couple of bread rolls and some salami,' Demelza said, quickly. 'I hadn't anticipated coming out for a full-blown picnic.'

Nick smiled. 'Don't worry. I've brought enough for an army. When I'm leaving the village each morning, I've got so many friends and relatives who're convinced I don't eat enough that I have to take extra bags

to put the food in. Ianni goes to school laden with
home-made pastries to share with his friends. I usually
share mine among the hospital staff so, as you can
imagine, both Ianni and I are very popular. I haven't
had time to open up my goodies this morning so I'm
glad you came along to help me eat it all.'

They were already walking down towards the sparkling blue sea. The sand was impossibly hot under
Demelza's feet.

'Ow!' She began to run the last few steps into the
sea.

Nick laughed as he streaked ahead. 'I always went
barefoot as a child whenever I could and the soles of
my feet are as hard as nails.'

Demelza felt nothing but relief as her feet touched
the cool water.

'The sea is amazingly cool, Nick,' she called as she
waded out towards the deeper water. 'I always thought
the Mediterranean would be warm.'

'The sea doesn't warm up until later in the summer.
Most Greeks say the sea is too cool to swim in before
August. But I'm half-English so I take my life in my
hands and swim when the tourists do, in the spring.'

'So you're half-English?' Demelza felt she wasn't
prying now that Nick had brought up the subject.

They were treading water, out of their depth, but the
salty Mediterranean was so buoyant it required little
effort to stay afloat.

He moved nearer to her, his strong, dark, muscular,
bare arm almost touching her pale white skin.

'Yes, my mother was English. She came out here
when she was a young student, fell in love with the
island and then with my father. I don't know which
love was stronger, because it broke her heart to leave

the island—mine, too, but I was only a child and more adaptable.'

'Why did you have to leave?' she asked carefully, as she turned onto her back with her eyes closed, allowing the buoyant water to hold her up.

Demelza felt as if she were lying on a water mattress. A small fish was tickling her toes. She spread her arms out from her sides, her fingers lazily stroking the surface of the water. The sun on her face felt so blissful. There wasn't a sound to be heard except the occasional bleat of a goat on the hillside and the gentle lapping of the water as she and Nick made languid movements with their limbs.

She heard Nick, beside her, drawing in his breath. For a few moments he didn't reply to her question. When he did, his voice was quiet, devoid of all emotion.

'My mother had to return to England…for medical reasons. So I had to go with her. It's a long story. Anyway, let's finish our swim. I'm starving!'

She heard the deliberate return to an animated tone. It was obvious that Nick didn't want to talk about it and, lying here in this idyllic paradise, she didn't want to hear anything that would change the atmosphere.

'I'm starving, too!' she said, quickly turning onto her front before setting off back. 'Race you to the shore!'

Nick broke into a strong crawl and streaked past her. He waited for her on the sand. He held out both his hands towards her as she emerged from the sea, and it seemed perfectly natural to take hold of them. She looked up into his eyes and gave a shiver.

'You're cold,' he said in a concerned tone. 'Come and dry yourself.'

She wasn't in the least bit cold. It had been the touch

of his hands that had produced the involuntary shiver. Whatever was the matter with her? She didn't dare to think.

She took a towel from her bag and went behind a tree to strip off and put on her spare bikini. This one was black and she'd only tried it on in the shop. The top was a little bit risqué, leaving not very much to the imagination, but the shop assistant had assured her it was what was being worn this year on Mediterranean beaches.

She'd felt decidedly daring to even consider a bikini in the first place, but the old swimsuit she'd had for more years than she cared to remember was literally falling to pieces. And when she'd investigated at the shop in the nearest town to the farm, the shop assistant had been adamant that she would be much too hot in a one-piece on a Mediterranean beach. Apparently, her over-helpful adviser had been on lots of package tours to the Med and knew what was required. So Demelza had emerged from the shop with two expensive bikinis, having spent an enormous amount on four very small strips of material.

She shielded her eyes as she looked up at the hot sun. Her skin was already dry and she felt more comfortable in a dry bikini. Nick, she noticed, was standing in the hot sun, towelling himself dry and slipping into dry shorts. She caught a glimpse of the brown skin at the top of his muscular legs and hurriedly averted her eyes. Her pulses were racing enough already!

Nick's dry shorts were black, like the other pair. She was now resigned to the effect they had on her and sauntered out from behind the tree as if she were used to taking lunch on a deserted beach with a handsome man she'd only met the day before.

'A glass of wine, Demelza?' Nick was uncorking a bottle.

'Lovely!'

She was going to suspend judgement on her wayward behaviour until the end of the meal. Sitting down on the rug, she smiled her thanks as she accepted the glass and took a tentative sip. Mmm! The wine was most refreshing. She leaned back on one elbow as she sipped.

Nick was smiling down at her. 'I think you're beginning to relax and get used to life on our island, aren't you, Demelza?'

She nodded and took another sip as she wiggled her toes in the sand at the end of the rug.

'Last night you seemed very nervous,' Nick said slowly. 'I wasn't sure you would fit into such an easygoing place, but now…'

She sat up straight, so that her eyes were closer to his. 'I've been out in the cold for such a long time that I find it hard…' She paused, searching for the right words. 'I find it hard to relate to people…especially men.'

'Ah! So that's the problem, is it?' He narrowed his eyes. 'Have you had a bad experience with men?'

'No, no! Quite the reverse. I've loved…too much… but always the same man, and now…'

He leaned forward. 'Love is very precious, isn't it? And when it's gone, how can you replace it?'

His voice was husky with emotion. She swallowed hard as she watched him straightening up before leaning back on his own side of the rug. For a brief, mad moment she'd imagined he was going to kiss her. And the idea that this could happen had been extremely pleasant…more than pleasant. She knew that it would have been an experience she would have enjoyed enormously.

But she realised that she'd completely overestimated Nick's intentions. She'd already witnessed that he was a kind, caring doctor, so he was merely giving her sympathy. But, oh, the touch of his lips would have meant so much more to her!

Nick seemed totally unaware of the emotional turmoil he'd caused as he reached out to remove packages from his large bag.

'Try one of these spinach pies. Anna makes the best spanokopita on the island.'

'Who's Anna?' Demelza asked as she bit into the flaky pastry. 'Mmm! This is delicious!'

'Anna is my aunt, my father's sister. She's married to Giorgio who owns the taverna. You may remember seeing her in the kitchen last night. She was busy cooking so there wasn't time to introduce you. Anyway, last night I didn't know you well enough to make a proper introduction.'

Demelza wiped the crumbs of the spanokopita from her lips with a paper napkin. 'Do you think you know me well enough now to introduce me to your aunt?'

He gave her a strange, enigmatic smile. 'I think the real you is hiding behind an iron curtain but I also think I've had a few glimpses of what you're really like. Maybe if you told me something about yourself, I'd get a better picture.'

Was she really hiding her real self? It was a startling thought, but Nick was probably right.

She took a sip of her wine and leaned back on her elbows. The fir tree they were picnicking under was providing some welcome shade and the view of the sea with the sun shining on it was breathtaking. She could feel herself relaxing even more.

'It's so long since I thought about myself as a person in my own right that sometimes I wonder who I really am. Since Simon died, I've simply looked after other people. I was so grief-stricken after his death that I didn't have the strength to see what was happening.'

'And what was happening?' he asked quietly.

She took a deep breath. 'The day that Simon was killed, I wanted to die as well.'

'He was killed?'

Nick's startled yet sympathetic voice gave her the strength to confront her fear of talking about the awful day that had changed her life for ever. She'd never actually used the word 'killed' before in connection with Simon's death…but that's what had happened. And the unexpectedness of it all had plunged her into deep shock.

'It was four months after our wedding. I was three months pregnant—very happily pregnant. Simon and I felt as if we were in heaven. We'd wanted to start a family—a large family—as soon as possible, and our wish had come true.'

Demelza cleared her throat. It seemed important to tell Nick the whole story, not just the bare outline which was what she usually came up with when it was absolutely essential to tell someone about Simon's death.

'Simon's last day started just like any other. He went out early to supervise the milking with a couple of farmhands. He always came back for breakfast afterwards and we would sit at the table and plan our day together…'

She broke off. 'I don't know why I'm telling you all the details. You don't want to know…'

'Oh, but I do!'

His strong voice reassured her again. Looking across into those dark, expressive eyes, she knew that she'd found a true friend.

'Take your time, Demelza,' he said huskily. 'I think it's good for you to relive the past. It can have a healing effect on your sadness.'

She nodded as she recognised that he was speaking as an experienced doctor again, a doctor who was used to listening to his patients. But she also knew that he was the sort of man in whom she could confide in a way she hadn't been able to since Simon's death.

'I remember, I got up to have my shower after Simon left, and then I went downstairs to prepare breakfast. I was lifting out a box of eggs from the cupboard when I heard the most alarming shouting going on outside the cowshed. I was still holding the eggs as I looked out of the window and saw… I remember my hands simply stopped working and the box of eggs slipped onto the kitchen floor…'

Demelza put her hands over her face. She didn't want Nick to see the uncontrollable tears. Gently, he moved to her side, carefully parting her hands with his own as he dabbed her face with a tissue.

'Don't be afraid to cry, Demelza. You've stored up this awful memory for a long time.' He paused before speaking quietly. 'What did you see?'

She swallowed hard, leaning back to prop herself against Nick's comforting shoulder. His strong arm was supporting both of them as they leaned close together on the rug.

'I saw Simon lying on the ground, partially covered

by the tractor which our youngest farmhand had reversed over him. I ran outside, but there was nothing anyone could do. I knew as I knelt over him that he was dead. I won't go into details, but all the clinical signs... I tried to revive him but I knew it was hopeless, even though I kept on until the ambulance arrived and...' She broke off, unable to go on.

Gently, Nick put his arms round her and held her close against his strong muscular chest.

'Cry if you want to, Demelza,' he said softly. 'Let it all come out. You need to get rid of all that grief.'

Her sobs were subsiding as she leaned against him. And for the first time in six years she felt a sense of calm stealing over her.

She pulled herself gently away so that she could look up into those dark, comforting eyes.

'Thank you, Nick,' she whispered. 'Thank you for listening so sympathetically. I think maybe I just glimpsed some light at the end of the tunnel.'

'I hope so, because I think I just glimpsed the real you. The woman behind the mask. Did you have any family to support you?' he asked gently.

'My own parents had died a couple of years before that. They'd been on a touring holiday when their coach crashed and unfortunately...'

She took another deep breath as the memories flooded back.

'Simon's family begged me to stay on at the farm. His parents said they couldn't manage without me, which was certainly true. They came to rely on me for everything. Soon I was running the farm and I couldn't see any way out of my... I don't want to seem melodramatic, but it used to feel as if I was serving a prison sentence. There was so much emotional blackmail from

Simon's mother that sometimes I felt I couldn't take on any more dutiful tasks.'

'You said you were three months pregnant when Simon died,' he said. 'What...?'

'I lost the baby at six months,' she said, in the even tone she always employed when it was essential to talk about her miscarriage. 'A scan had showed my baby was a boy. He was the only thing that kept me going immediately after Simon's death. And then, when he was gone, I simply lived from day to day. But last year Simon's younger brother got married and his wife wanted to live with him at the farm.'

'So you saw a way out after all that time?' Nick said, gently.

Demelza made an effort to smile. 'I saw an escape route and I took it.'

What would Nick think of her, crying like that? But it was his encouragement that had prompted her to open up. She felt a lifting of her spirits. He was going to be a good friend.

Perhaps more than a friend? She knew she was certainly attracted to Nick. It was more than mere admiration at the sight of his handsome, muscular frame. It wasn't the fact that she was starved of love and affection—even though that certainly was true. No, it was pure, unadulterated attraction for Nick, the man himself. But how would she react if their friendship moved on? She'd had so little experience of men in social situations. In fact, she was a complete novice! It was wonderful to think of becoming involved with Nick, but at the same time she was afraid she wouldn't be able to cope.

She reached for her wineglass, which had fallen over in the sand.

'Do you think I could have another glass of wine?'

Nick smiled. 'You most certainly can.'

She watched his strong, firm fingers as he reached across with the bottle. He would make an excellent surgeon, she was sure of it.

'Where did you train as a doctor?' she asked, raising the glass to her lips.

He propped the bottle up against a stone and turned to face her. 'In London, at St Celine's hospital.'

'And you prefer to work out here?'

He smiled. 'Don't you? Is there any comparison between living on a dark London street and spending your days on this warm sunny island?'

She moved to the edge of the rug and propped herself up against the sun-warmed smooth surface of a large rock. 'You're absolutely right. There's absolutely no comparison.'

'Come on, you've hardly eaten anything! Catch!' Nick picked up a ripe, juicy tomato and tossed it in her direction.

Demelza laughed as she caught it.

'And then you must try some of this cheese pie that Anna made. We call it theropita.'

'Theropita,' Demelza said carefully. 'I've brought a teach-yourself-Greek book with me, but I haven't had much time to study it yet.'

'I can teach you,' Nick said.

'I'd like that,' she said softly, knowing that she would enjoy any activity that brought her into contact with Nick.

From somewhere amongst the pile of Nick's clothes a phone was ringing. He pulled a mobile from his trouser pocket.

Demelza heard him speaking in rapid Greek, his face

stern and concentrated as he listened. He cut the connection and stood up.

'That was Nurse Krisanthe. She's admitted a young woman who's about thirty-five weeks pregnant. Apparently, she's been in labour at home for several hours and hadn't realised what was happening. The foetus is showing signs of distress and Nurse Krisanthe thinks a Caesarean section might be necessary.'

Nick was pulling his trousers on over his shorts. Demelza leapt to her feet and began extricating her dress from her bag.

'Have you got the necessary staff for a Caesarean?' she asked after she'd buttoned up the front of her dress over her bikini. They were already trekking back over the sand, Nick's long legs outstripping her so that she had to take two strides to his one.

'I've told Krisanthe to contact our anaesthetist and have him standing by. I'll perform the Caesarean if it's necessary. I may find it possible to deliver the baby naturally, but I won't know until I've examined the patient.'

'But if the baby is displaying obvious signs of distress then the sooner we get the baby out the better,' she said, breathlessly climbing into the Land Rover beside Nick.

'Yes, yes, of course,' he said, a trifle irritably.

All trace of her relaxed companion of the last couple of hours had disappeared. Nick was totally focussed now on the medical task in hand. She'd better confine her remarks to the minimum.

Nick gripped the steering-wheel hard as he drove the rugged vehicle up the hill. Demelza tried not to think about the sheer drop at the side of the bumpy road as she stared straight ahead.

'I believe you've had experience in obstetrics, haven't you?' Nick said tersely.

'Yes. I staffed in Obstetrics Theatre for a while. We—'

'Would you assist me today? My obstetrics sister is off sick and I don't want to call her back until she's completely recovered.'

'Of course I'll assist.' Demelza knew she was very experienced but she felt a little scared. She tried to convince herself that her practical and theoretical training wouldn't desert her. You never lost the medical and surgical skills that you'd practised over the years, did you?

'Good!' Nick flashed her a grateful smile and her spirits lifted. It would be good to take on some real nursing after all this time.

She thought about the patient waiting for them to arrive as Nick increased his speed when they reached the metalled road. The sooner they could get back to the hospital the better.

A young nurse was waiting for them in Reception. Her face broke into a relieved smile as they arrived.

'Come quickly, Dr Capodistrias!'

They followed the slight, white-clad figure down the corridor to the obstetrics ward. Nurse Krisanthe was leaning over her patient, wiping a damp cloth over her brow. The young father-to-be was sitting beside the bed, holding tightly to his wife's hand. He looked up in relief when Nick arrived, and began a torrent of agitated words.

'Michaelis tells me that Katia, his wife, has been experiencing pain since the middle of last night but they had no idea she was in labour,' Nick told Demelza as they scrubbed up before examining their patient.

Demelza was alarmed to see that the dilatation of the cervix was very poor. They couldn't deliver the baby until the birth canal was much wider. Meantime, glancing at the foetal monitor, it was obvious that the baby was suffering acute distress. It needed to be delivered as soon as possible.

'We haven't time to try dilating the cervix with drugs,' Nick said evenly. 'I'm going to take Katia into Theatre.'

A small man came hurrying through the swing doors. 'This is Dr Patris, our anaesthetist,' Nick told Demelza. He spoke briefly to the man before outlining what was happening to the young mother and her anxious husband.

There was no time for the usual pre-operative preparations. Without any preamble, the patient was wheeled into the small operating theatre and anaesthetised.

A young nurse dressed Demelza in a sterile gown. As she stood at the other side of the table from Nick she felt her strength and confidence returning. She'd been in similar situations many times before. Her skills were still intact. Carefully, she swabbed the patient's abdomen before handing Nick a scalpel in preparation for the incision.

Nick leaned across their patient and carefully cut through the abdominal wall and into the lower segment of the uterus. He paused briefly before placing his gloved hands in the cavity and removing the baby.

Demelza had seen this performed many times but it never ceased to move her. The sight of a newborn infant, saved by Caesarean section, was always miraculous to her. Without their intervention, the baby would have had very little chance of survival.

'It's a girl!' Nick said, his eyes smiling above the mask as he clamped and cut the umbilical cord.

Demelza looked across at him and felt a rush of happiness. Her happiness was momentarily tinged with sadness as she remembered her own son. But only momentarily. She wouldn't allow any morbid thoughts to spoil the moment. She was a professional again and, as such, there was no time for self-pity.

'Nothing wrong with her lungs!' she remarked as she took the lustily bawling infant from Nick's hands and carried her over to the nearby examination table. Carefully, she cleaned the wrinkled newborn, wrapping her in a sterile dressing sheet before beginning the routine postnatal checks. When Nick had finished treating the mother he came across to check the baby's heart and lungs.

'No obvious complications, Demelza. We've been very lucky here. I think young Katia got her dates muddled up. She hasn't been into hospital for any antenatal check-ups. She told me she thought she was about thirty-five weeks pregnant, but I would say she was nearer full term. What's the birth weight?'

'Three and a half kilos. Not bad for a first baby.'

Nick smiled down at her. 'Definitely full term, I would say.'

He lowered his voice. 'I remember Katia's and Michaelis's wedding about six months ago. Since then, I've had the distinct impression Katia has been avoiding me in the village. These things still matter out here. It's such a pity she put the baby's life at risk. Katia and Michaelis are both only seventeen, so they're still very much under parental control. I may have to corroborate a fib to her grandmother and say that Katia's baby came early.'

Demelza smiled. 'Are you willing to do that?'

'If a little white lie will keep the family happy I'm willing to go along with the general conspiracy, even though I know Grandma will have her own theory when she sees the large baby with her lovely black hair and long nails.'

'I can see I've got a lot to learn about the customs on Kopelos.'

'Plenty of time,' Nick said, as he watched her wrapping the newborn girl in a cotton sleeping gown.

'I've only got six months out here,' she said slowly, as she lifted the baby into her arms. The warmth of this newborn miracle brought a lump to her throat, which she swallowed rapidly. No looking back now. She was going forward.

'Ah, yes, I'd forgotten how short your contract was. As it's a new venture, the travel company want to make sure there is a need for this new clinic. The beach resort closes down in the winter months. Well, thank you very much for your help. If you'd like to escort mother and baby back to the ward, I'll see them shortly when I've finished my rounds.'

Demelza held the baby against her as she watched Nick striding out of the theatre. She'd been dismissed and she should feel relieved that her work was finished. But she didn't. She and Nick were back on professional terms again. It was as if the picnic on the beach had been a dream.

As she stood outside the hospital a short time later, she knew she was free to go, but she felt reluctant to leave. The evening stretched ahead of her and she felt suddenly at a loose end. The sun was already dipping lower in the sky and the islanders were preparing to socialise. Across the road from the hospital she could see a group of old men sitting outside at a table, having a loud discussion as they sipped their glasses of ouzo.

She ought to make the effort to join in somewhere, find out more about the fascinating culture of this island. She felt a sense of loss stealing over her and knew she would have to pull herself together. There was a sense of anticlimax after the excitement of the emergency Caesarean. That was what was hitting her now, she told herself unconvincingly.

In her heart of hearts she knew that it was more than that. Since midday she'd been with Nick, roused by his enthusiasm for life, encouraged by his *joie de vivre*. And she missed him already, although it was only about an hour since they'd parted in Theatre.

She'd just been another pair of willing hands to him and she shouldn't take him too seriously. In this re-awakening process he was the first man who'd stirred any interest in her.

She was a complete novice again where emotions were concerned and she had a lot to learn about not going overboard. She looked along the road that led to the village. It couldn't be much more than a mile. The walk would do her good and she might snap out of this dreadful mood that had claimed her.

Walking along the road, her spirits began to lift again. It was difficult not to get the feel-good factor when you started to absorb the atmosphere of this vibrant island. She passed a couple of tavernas where the evening socialising was developing. The haunting strains of Greek music followed her along the road and she found herself smiling.

So much had changed since she'd met Nick. He was good to look at, wonderful company in an off-duty situation. It was a relief to find that her interest in the opposite sex was re-emerging. But could she cope with the emotional turmoil that was already making itself obvious?

She jumped to the side of the road in alarm as a vehicle ground to a halt beside her.

'Sorry, I didn't mean to scare you!'

Nick was leaning across, holding open the passenger door of his Land Rover. 'Can I give you a lift back to the village?'

She hesitated. Having admitted her confused feelings about Nick, she knew it might be safer to say she preferred to walk. But that just wasn't true and, anyway, Nick would wonder why she was spurning his offer.

'Thanks.' She climbed up into the passenger seat. 'I was actually enjoying the walk.'

'I'm sure you were, but I wanted to talk to you. I'd hoped to catch you before you left the hospital but my rounds took longer than usual. I do like to get home as early as I can for Ianni. Katerina is very good with him but I know he's happiest when I'm home.'

'I'm sure he is. What about his mother? Doesn't he miss her?'

Nick hesitated, his eyes firmly fixed on the road ahead. A donkey ambled out of an alley and wandered onto the road. Nick slowed until the donkey's owner had got the animal under control again.

'Ianni has got used to our life being just the two of us. It was an acrimonious divorce and I think, young as he was, Ianni soaked up some of the unpleasant atmosphere. It was a relief for him when everything became resolved and the two of us had a home together away from Lydia.'

Demelza recognised the emotional overtones in Nick's voice and decided it wouldn't be fair to pry.

Nick would tell her more if he wanted to. And it was really none of her business, she reminded herself. She was trying very hard to remain detached from Nick's affairs.

'I'm sure it was a difficult experience for both you and Ianni,' she said, quietly.

'You're absolutely right, Demelza. I couldn't go through that again.'

He gave a harsh laugh. 'In fact, if I'm honest, I'd run a mile if I ever felt I was going to commit myself to a scheming woman again.'

'Was she scheming—your ex-wife?'

In spite of her better judgement, Demelza found her curiosity was getting the better of her. And was it her imagination, or did she feel that Nick was relieved to be able to talk to her? Just as she'd found it helpful to talk to him about her past life when they'd been on the beach that afternoon.

It was nothing to do with her interest in the man, she tried to tell herself. She was merely providing a willing, sympathetic ear.

'Tell me about it!' Nick said, his voice full of emotion. 'You name it, Lydia tried it on.'

He paused. 'Funny thing was, as soon as we'd settled custody of Ianni, it became easier.'

He broke off and smiled. 'Talk of the devil!' He pulled the vehicle to a halt at the entrance to the narrow village street where motorised vehicles were prohibited. The street was only wide enough for motorbikes and Demelza had learned that even they had been banned when they'd become too much of a nuisance.

'See what I see?' Nick said, pointing down between the ancient houses of the narrow street.

Two little boys were chasing each other outside one

of the houses, whooping with laughter. As Nick reversed his car into the parking space at the end of the street, Ianni looked in their direction.

'Daddy!' the little boy shouted happily.

Lefteris, his little friend, was completely forgotten as Ianni charged down the street to meet his father.

'I was waiting for you, Daddy. Katerina said it was too soon but...'

Ianni flung himself into Nick's arms. Nick hugged him closely, a contented smile on his face.

'Remember Demelza?'

Ianni smiled. 'Of course.' The young boy moved around the front of the car and held up his arms towards her.

Demelza knelt down, smiling happily as Ianni hugged her, not so enthusiastically as with his father but certainly showing that she was his friend.

'Are you coming to Giorgio's with us again, Demel...Demelza?' Ianni asked, his young, beguiling eyes shining with innocent excitement.

'Well, I—'

Nick's mobile rang. She was glad of the interruption. There was nothing she would like better than to immerse herself in this family situation but she was so afraid of overstepping the mark...and so afraid of becoming too involved. Far better to make her excuses sooner rather than later.

She glanced at Nick who was having an earnest conversation in Greek. He looked worried as he ended the call.

'I've just agreed to go back to the hospital,' he said to Demelza. 'Katia is complaining of abdominal pain. I have to check her out. The thing is...' He was glancing down at Ianni who was frowning. 'I'm sorry, Ianni.

You'd better stay on with Katerina for a bit longer. I'll be as quick as I can.'

'Can't I go home and be with Demelza?' Ianni asked plaintively. 'She lives upstairs and...I could get my homework done, couldn't I?'

Nick's face creased into a grin. 'You really are a manipulative little—'

'Don't worry about Ianni,' Demelza heard herself saying. 'I'll take care of him till you get back.' She glanced down at Ianni who had wrapped his arms around her legs in gratitude. 'But it's homework first, remember?'

Ianni grinned and said something to Lefteris, obviously indicating that they'd finished their game. Demelza felt the little boy's hand taking hold of hers. It was a wonderful feeling to be wanted like this.

'Well, if you're sure,' Nick said. 'I'll call in and tell Katerina where Ianni is, and if you want to go out, Katerina will be willing to—'

'Stop worrying. I'm perfectly happy to look after Ianni.'

'Go on, Dad!' Ianni said. 'The sooner you go, the sooner you'll get back, and there might still be time for us all to go to Giorgio's.'

As Demelza's eyes met Nick's she was thinking that young Ianni was old beyond his years. He'd probably suffered over the divorce of his parents but it didn't seem to have done him any harm.

'See you later,' Nick called as he reversed the car and went back along the road to the town.

Ianni was tugging her impatiently. 'Come on, Demelza.'

Her plans for the evening were now mapped out. Everything was beyond her control, but she found herself happily looking forward to the next few hours. Looking after Nick's child wasn't becoming too involved, was it? It wasn't as if she'd actively sought to become involved in this family. It had just sort of happened. But she hadn't felt so light-hearted in a long time. Not since...

She didn't want to think about how long it was since she'd felt so happy. It was merely a release of the emotions she'd kept cooped up. That and the effect of the warm sun and the sparkling blue sea. It was like taking a holiday from herself. She would have felt like this even without the comfort of this ready-made family, wouldn't she?

CHAPTER FOUR

DEMELZA was sitting on the edge of Nick's sofa, trying desperately to keep her eyes open, when Nick returned from the hospital. The small pyjama-clad figure in her arms stirred at the sound of his father's voice, but his eyes remained closed.

Nick sat down beside her on the sofa. 'I'm sorry I took so long, Demelza. As I said, when I phoned you from the hospital, it wasn't a straightforward case. If I hadn't known Katia's background I wouldn't have been able to sort out what was happening.'

He leaned back against the sofa and closed his eyes wearily. 'Katia was insisting she had these terrible abdominal pains and it was only when I called her bluff and said I would have to take her back to Theatre that she admitted she wasn't in pain. She was desperately worried about her family's reaction to her baby arriving too soon after the wedding.'

'So what did she hope to achieve?' Demelza whispered, shifting the position of the little boy in her arms.

Nick leaned forward and picked up Ianni, cradling him over his shoulder and whispering soothing noises. 'I'll put Ianni into his bed and tell you all about it.'

'He wanted to see you before he slept,' Demelza said softly, 'so I thought, as he didn't know me very well, I wouldn't insist on putting him to bed.'

Nick nodded. 'Back in a moment.'

He was carrying a bottle of wine and two glasses

when he returned. 'Ianni's fast asleep. Would you like a glass of wine?'

She nodded. 'Yes, please. Strange how easy it is to slip into the sun, sea and wine culture. I can't believe I've only been here a couple of days.'

Nick laughed as he handed her a glass. 'You'll be a proper native by the end of the summer. You look different already...sort of more relaxed, as if you're blossoming in the sun like the flowers.'

Demelza tried to stop herself from blushing but she could feel the heat on her cheeks as she met Nick's gaze.

'I certainly feel as if I've survived a long cold winter and suddenly been brought out into the sun,' she said.

He reached forward and gently touched her cheek. 'Yes, I can see the colour in your cheeks already. You've been starved of all the things that make life worth living for far too long, but now...' He spread his hands wide as if to indicate that all things were possible.

She could feel a magical tingling of her skin where his fingers had touched her face as he clinked his glass against hers.

'Thank you very much for looking after Ianni. He seems to have taken a shine to you. He's happy enough with Katerina but she can be a bit too bossy for his liking. I think I've probably spoiled him since his mother and I split up. Anyway, I was going to tell you about our patient, Katia,' he hurried on, as if reluctant to dwell on thoughts of his wife.

'Was Katia really putting on an act simply to get your attention?' Demelza asked.

'She was pretty convincing at first, but when I'd examined her thoroughly I started to have my suspicions.

Just to give her some peace of mind, I've said that if I meet her grandmother I won't deny that the baby was early.'

Demelza was shaking her head in disbelief. 'I can't believe it matters. As you say, I've got a lot to learn about life on Kopelos. How is the baby?'

Nick smiled. 'Thriving. Katia's feeding him, lying down because that's more comfortable after a Caesarean, and there are no problems there.'

'That's great,' she smiled back, realising that for the first time, it didn't hurt to talk about babies. She drew in a breath, aware that Nick was watching her closely. She felt as if she'd achieved another milestone and she wondered if he knew.

She put down her glass as she thought how nice it was to chat with Nick at the end of a long day. This was something she'd missed when Simon had no longer been there. Simple companionship. Simon's parents had begged her to stay in the sitting room with them during the evening, ostensibly to talk but more often merely to be another person watching the endless television until it was time for her to heat the milk for their bedtime drinks.

'You've got that far-away look again,' Nick said quietly. 'Are you getting homesick?'

Demelza laughed. 'You must be joking! No, I was just wondering how Mark and Jane are coping with life on the farm. I hope Jane isn't getting fed up with the constant demands of the family.'

'Well, as you say, you served your time. And it will be easier for your sister-in-law because she has her husband to help her. You were on your own and suffering the double sorrow of losing your husband and your son.'

She leaned back against the sofa and smiled. 'I'm glad you said that. Between the sorrow and the dutiful demands I found it hard to think straight sometimes about where I was going to end up.'

'And where are you going to end up?' Nick asked gently, as he moved across to top up her glass, staying beside her on the sofa, one arm stretched along the back.

She laughed. 'I'm probably going to end up feeling quite woozy if I drink any more wine. Let's say, I'm not looking too far ahead in the future at the moment. It's enough that I've escaped to live my own life.'

He nodded. 'I know how you feel. It felt like an escape when I finally got away from England, Lydia and the divorce and started a new life out here with Ianni. All I want from now on is a life free from personal complications.'

She felt Nick's arm move along the sofa behind her. She turned to look at him and was touched by the plaintive expression in his eyes. Yes, he, too, had suffered a great deal and was now enjoying his freedom.

'It's good to feel that I've found a friend with the same outlook on life,' she said, quietly.

Gently, his fingers closed over her shoulder and he pulled her gently towards him. She felt her body responding to his touch. Wasn't this a dangerous move for friends to be making? Slowly, he bent his head and kissed her lips very gently.

Moments later, the kiss was over. She moved to pull herself away and he let her go, a tender smile playing on his sensual lips.

'Don't be afraid, Demelza. I meant that to be a friendly kiss.'

'I know,' she said quickly. 'We both know where we stand on friendship, don't we?'

'I thought we did,' he said carefully.

Now, what had Nick meant by that? Had their kiss had as devastating an effect on him as it had had on her?

Demelza stood up. 'It's time for me to go. I had a call on my mobile from Irini, the nurse who assists me at the beach resort, reminding me that we've got an early clinic tomorrow.'

He was standing looking down at her, once more merely the friend and medical colleague. Her knees felt weak and wobbly as she looked at the rugged features surrounding the mouth that had just kissed hers, causing such an unnerving reaction deep down inside her. He was tall, very tall. She was aware that he towered over her and she had long legs herself. She was also aware of his strong muscular arms beneath the thin cotton shirt, arms which she suddenly ached to have close around her.

'Well, thanks again for looking after Ianni,' he said.

'My pleasure,' she said, knowing that she'd enjoyed every minute of taking care of such a delightful young boy.

The fact that he was Nick's son wasn't influencing the way she felt about Ianni. She was trying to remain detached from the little boy in the same way that she was trying not to allow her attraction towards his father to distract her too much.

He stood at the door of his apartment as she climbed the stone steps to her apartment. The moonlight was strong enough to light her way and there was an outside light over her door which she'd put on when she'd first got back with Ianni. The little boy had been intrigued by her apartment and had asked if he could come up to see her another day. She'd insisted he must ask his father first, and had hoped fervently that Nick would say yes. There was nothing she would like better than young Ianni playing around her apartment and sun terrace.

She paused at the top of the stone stairs and leaned over to call, 'Goodnight!'

Nick waved a hand. 'Goodnight. Sleep well!'

Oh, she would sleep well tonight! It had been such a memorable day. Memorable and enjoyable, nothing more than that.

She closed the door and leaned against it, breathing heavily. She tried to convince herself that nothing had changed. Nick had said he wanted an uncomplicated life and so did she. Well, to a certain extent! The memory of Nick's kiss was having a devastating effect on her.

As she stripped off her clothes and sat down in front of the small, wooden dressing-table she was still trying to calm her confused thoughts. She picked up her hairbrush and vigorously stroked through her long auburn hair. Watching herself in the mirror, she could see the excitement still dancing in her green eyes, eyes that had held a dead expression for far too long.

It's all part of the breaking-out process, she told herself. Coming to life again after years of lying dormant. Nick had called it blossoming. That was such a lovely idea! And it would have happened even without meeting Nick...wouldn't it?

No, she wouldn't have felt like this! But Nick, with his own complicated life, wouldn't want her as anything more than a friend. Or would he? How was she to interpret his tender kiss? When a mere friend kissed you it shouldn't cause such havoc with your emotions.

As she tried to sleep the confusion of her feelings for Nick continued to plague her and she realised once more how inexperienced she was with relationships. She'd only ever had one man in her life. So getting to know Nick was like taking a step in the dark.

Demelza had a busy morning at the clinic. As she'd predicted the day before when she'd looked out at the tourists stretched out on their sunbeds, soaking up the sun with insufficient protection, there were several people suffering today. Fortunately, there was no one bad enough to require hospitalisation, although one fair-haired girl had come pretty close.

'You'd better stay inside for the next few days, Jenny,' Demelza said, as she applied lotion to the most badly affected areas.

'But I'm only out here for a week,' the young woman said. 'That's why I was trying to get a tan quickly.'

'It doesn't work like that,' Demelza told her patient. 'A suntan takes time and lots of protection. You can't rush it or you end up looking like a lobster and feeling as if you've been boiled alive.'

Jenny pulled a face. 'Next time, I suppose I'd better start off with a strong sunblock and come out here for a longer time.'

Demelza nodded. 'That's the only way to do it. Or you could apply a fake tan and sit under the umbrella. Fake tans from reputable cosmetic firms are perfectly safe—but not this time,' she added quickly. 'Your skin's too damaged at the moment.'

It was a surprise to see that her next patient was

Bryony Driver, the woman suffering from depression that she'd seen only the day before.

'Hello, Bryony. Hadn't expected to see you back so soon. How are you?'

Bryony slowly settled herself in the patient's chair, giving Demelza the impression that she had plenty of time to spare—unlike herself! She could hear the hum of voices outside in the waiting room but was well aware that she had to give her patient a few minutes at least. But she hoped it wasn't going to turn out to be a lengthy consultation. The patients suffering from depression that she'd treated during her professional life had all taken up a lot of time. There was no quick route back to normality.

'I've gone back on my pills but I had a terrible night, Sister,' Bryony said, in a dull tone. 'Tossing and turning and—'

'Did you read a book like I suggested, yesterday?'

'I couldn't concentrate. It was a love story and I couldn't stop thinking about Vinny, wondering if he was in bed with that scheming little minx and...'

Demelza let her patient ramble on for a while, going over the same ground they'd covered previously. One thing that alarmed her was that, although it was only just after nine o'clock in the morning, there was a definite smell of alcohol on Bryony's breath. When there was a pause long enough to break in, Demelza carefully tackled the question.

'You do know you mustn't drink alcohol with the pills you're taking, don't you, Bryony?'

Bryony's eyes widened as she stared across at Demelza. 'Sister, I wouldn't dream of abusing alcohol.' She paused. 'Well, I might have had a little nip of brandy in the middle of the night when I was feeling so desperate, but—'

'And again this morning perhaps?' Demelza said.

Bryony nodded sheepishly. 'You don't know what it's like being me, Sister. Waking up each morning and having to face another day without—'

'You're right. I don't know what it's like to be you, Bryony,' Demelza said sympathetically. 'But I'm going to try and help you all I can.'

Her patient couldn't help the fact that she had other patients to see and that their current discussion was leading nowhere. Bryony needed to see a psychiatrist.

'I really think it might be better for you to go home, Bryony,' Demelza said carefully. 'You're not responding to the medication you're taking but I think if you talked over your problems with a good psychiatrist, then—'

'I don't want to go home. I'm all on my own in England. At least out here I can mix with other people when I want to. Aren't there any psychiatrists out here?'

'I'll make enquiries,' Demelza said. 'I'll get in touch with the hospital and let you know. Otherwise I really think you should—'

'I'm not going home.' Bryony rose to her feet, her eyes flashing defiantly. 'I feel awful out here but I felt even worse back home. When can you let me know about the psychiatrist?'

'Come and see me in a couple of days,' Demelza said quickly. 'Take care of yourself.'

She leaned back in her chair as Bryony went out, knowing that she could have picked up the phone and got the relevant information from the hospital. But she wanted time to discuss the case with Nick.

Her other patients that morning were all suffering from physical symptoms that could be treated with medication—coughs, colds, sore throats brought out from England but still lingering in spite of the sunshine. As the last patient left her consulting room, Demelza thought how much less complicated it was to treat the body than the mind. She felt out of her depth with Bryony.

Getting up from her chair, she looked out into the waiting room. Nobody there except Irini who was re-setting the trays and trolleys they'd used that morning.

'You can go when you've finished that, Irini. Thanks very much for your help.'

The girl smiled. Demelza was pleased to have such a willing assistant. Trained at a hospital in Athens, she was proving to be a valuable asset to the clinic. Back in her room, Demelza picked up the phone, dialled the hospital number and asked for Nick.

She hung on. Hearing the babble of Greek voices in the background, it reminded her that she would have to do something about learning the language. Nick had said he would help her but—

'Nick, it's Demelza,' she said when at last she heard his voice. 'I've got a patient with a bad case of depression. I think she needs to be seen by a psychiatrist but she's out here for a long time and doesn't want to go back to the UK. Is there a psychiatrist attached to the hospital?'

'We haven't got a full-time psychiatrist. There's a semi-retired doctor who still takes patients privately but he's not cheap.'

'I don't think consultation fees would be a problem, from what I've gathered from my patient. I'll check that out and if Bryony is still willing to be treated, perhaps you could arrange it for me.'

'Certainly. But you'll need to give me a few details—not over the phone. I'm busy right now. Perhaps you could call round this evening, Demelza?'

She felt her spirits lifting. 'Yes, I'll do that, Nick. Thanks a lot.'

Putting down the phone, she dialled Bryony's room number. Her patient seemed relieved that Demelza was treating her case so quickly and assured her that money wasn't a problem. As she'd said earlier, Vinny, her ex-husband, had given her a very generous settlement and she had no one to spend it on but herself.

Arriving back at the apartment, Demelza showered and changed into her bikini. She'd contemplated an afternoon on the beach but had decided that she had too many chores to see to at the apartment. And she could intersperse the washing, ironing and sorting out the apartment with a little cautious sunbathing on her terrace.

Looking over the balustrade, she saw that Nick's apartment was quite deserted. Just as well, she thought, because she wasn't entirely secluded from downstairs and although she hadn't felt out of place in her bikini on the beach, it was a different matter at the apartment. It was true she wasn't overlooked in any direction. The hillside sloped upwards to the craggy summit and only the goats and a few sheep cropping the sparse grass would be able to see what she was up to. But outside the door to the courtyard of the villa was a street of houses where the women were definitely well covered, regardless of the temperature.

She spread the things she'd washed on an airer in

the corner of the terrace where they would get maximum sunshine. It hadn't taken long to rinse out the washing which had accumulated since she'd left England and her apartment was looking reasonably neat and tidy now. A quick swipe around with the broom she'd found in a cupboard had sorted out the ancient stone floor. She'd shaken the brightly coloured rugs, one from her living room and one from her bedroom, and repositioned them.

The easiest session of housework she'd done in a long time, she thought as she stretched out on the sunbed under the umbrella. Mmm! This was the life!

The soothing drone of the insects on the hillside, creating a continuous lullaby, coupled with the heat from the sun, was getting to her. She closed her eyes, telling herself that she wasn't going to go to sleep because that would be a waste of an afternoon and she wanted to read the book she'd started on the plane so...

It was the clang of the gate that awoke her. She jumped up, feeling completely disorientated as she peered over the balustrade down into the courtyard. Her eyes widened.

'Nick! What time is it?'

Nick seemed amused by her confusion. 'I'm home early. It's only four o'clock. I didn't mean to disturb your siesta. You look as if you've been asleep.'

She glanced down at her semi-clad figure, feeling vulnerable. Nick had seen her in a bikini on the beach but here at the apartment she wasn't sure whether it would be frowned upon to be seen like this. Maybe it was totally inappropriate in this ancient part of the village.

But Nick certainly wasn't frowning. Her new emerging self pushed the ideas firmly to one side. She had to make the most of this wonderful sunshine because it would be very cold when she returned to an English winter at the end of her Greek summer.

'Would you like a drink?' she found herself asking, boldly and totally out of character. 'I've squeezed some oranges and the juice is chilling in the fridge.'

'Great! I need to strip off and have a shower first. Be with you in a few minutes.'

His dark eyes seemed to be lingering over her bikini-clad figure. Demelza suddenly felt that she was being terribly forward and wondered how she was going to handle it. Half of her was holding back and saying that she was going too quickly towards some unknown, unplanned destination.

She turned and made for the door to her apartment. 'I'll get the juice,' she called. 'And later, when you've recovered, we could perhaps discuss my patient, the one I told you about.'

She was deliberately trying to keep their relationship on a steady footing. Inviting Nick up for a drink was merely returning the hospitality he'd shown her since she'd arrived.

Returning with a jug of chilled juice, two glasses and the olives she'd bought at the local shop on her way home, she repositioned the umbrella over the table and sat bolt upright, waiting nervously. She'd tied a black and white sarong over her bikini and felt slightly less brazen.

Nick came bounding up the stairs. He was wearing khaki shorts but his chest was completely bare. Demelza groaned inwardly at the sight of his muscular body. She tried to convince herself that it was only natural that she should feel like this after festering in the backwoods for so long. She hadn't felt the slightest desire to notice what the farmhands looked like.

'Nice sarong!' Nick said, as he leaned across the table to accept a glass of orange juice. 'You didn't buy that out here, did you?'

'I got it in Cornwall, the same time I bought my bikinis. My mother-in-law asked to see what I'd bought and you should have seen her face!'

'She didn't approve?'

Demelza laughed. 'That's an understatement! She said she hoped I wasn't going to forget that I was a widow now that I was going to start living the high life.'

He was watching her over the rim of his glass as he sipped. 'I don't think you'll ever forget you're a widow, but it doesn't mean you can't enjoy yourself.'

'That's what I've started to tell myself,' she said quickly. 'I'll never forget Simon...but it's time to move on.'

Nick leaned towards her. 'Was Simon your first love?'

She nodded. 'We met at the village school. There was never anyone but Simon for me. When I went away to London to do my nursing training we always made a point of seeing each other as often as we could. Simon was at agricultural college for a couple of years and then he went back to work for his father on the farm. But during all that time and after I was trained we were never apart for more than a few weeks at a time.'

'Sounds like a real love match. You must have been very happy together.' He paused. 'I was happy with Lydia at the beginning, but it didn't last. We had a very short, whirlwind romance and didn't really get to know each other until after we were married.'

'How long were you married to Lydia?' Demelza asked gently.

He leaned back and attempted a weary smile.

'Too long. The only thing that kept us going was Ianni who was born at the end of our first year of marriage. Soon after he was born, Lydia started having a string of affairs. She'd found out that being married to a hard-working doctor and having to look after a child wasn't very glamorous. She gets bored very easily so she worked hard at making herself attractive to other men…preferably rich ones who could take her out and give her a good time.'

'When did you find out that Lydia was being unfaithful?'

He gave a harsh laugh. 'It became pretty obvious when she insisted on having a mother's help to take care of Ianni so that she could go out more. I was so busy in the hospital at the time that for a while I shelved the problem, but I made sure that the mother's help was taking good care of Ianni when I wasn't there.'

He paused and drew in a breath. 'I was trying to ride out the storm for Ianni's sake. I didn't want the family to break up, but we couldn't have gone on much longer like that. When Lydia asked me for a divorce it was a tremendous relief. She told me she'd found someone else richer and more interesting than a doctor who was always too busy at the hospital.'

He pulled a wry face. 'Those were Lydia's exact words, actually.'

'And is your ex-wife happy with this rich, interesting man?'

He raised a dark eyebrow. 'She was for a while, until he dumped her and took off with someone else. Poor Lydia! She came running back to me, begging me to have her back, but I told her it was too late for a reconciliation.'

He broke off and gave himself a little shake. 'Can't think why I'm telling you all this. Perhaps it's to show you that it didn't do you any harm to stay on at the farm and not go out into the world until you felt you were ready. You might have fallen for the first man who took you out of yourself, had a whirlwind romance and lived to regret it, as I did.'

'Oh, I wouldn't have done that,' she said quickly, as the little voice inside her warned her that this was exactly what was happening now.

But six years down the line, wasn't she strong enough to know what she was doing? Probably not, judging by the mixed emotions that were churning up inside her.

'More juice, Nick?' She picked up the jug, anxious to diffuse the emotional atmosphere. 'It's a bit warm now. I'll put some more ice in it.'

As she stood up, the knot in her sarong unravelled and it slipped to the floor. With a jug in one hand she could hardly reach down, pick up the sarong and retie it. Carefully, she stepped over it and walked barefoot across the warm paving stones and through the open door.

Her small kitchen seemed cool and dark after the brightness and warmth of the hot sun. She bent down and opened the fridge to pull out the ice tray. It was sticking to the surrounding ice. She tugged, before resorting to grabbing a knife from the draining board and trying to prise it out.

'Ouch!' She couldn't stifle a cry as her finger caught on the sharp corner of the tin ice tray. 'Of all the stupid contraptions…!'

She became aware that Nick was bending over her. 'Here, let me do that.'

He leaned inside the fridge and dislodged the tray with apparent ease.

'Your finger's bleeding!' Nick grabbed the first cloth that came to hand and wound it round her finger. 'This cloth is decidedly unsterile, but I think you'll live.'

'Thanks!' She was still crouching in front of the fridge inwardly cursing herself for being such an idiot and feeling intensely aware that she was wearing only a flimsy bikini.

Nick was still holding onto the cloth wrapped around her finger. His eyes were unnervingly near to her own…and his mouth! She held her breath as he bent his head slowly and placed a feather-light kiss on her finger.

Immediately, his head came up and he smiled into her eyes. 'That's only what I would do if Ianni had hurt his finger.'

She swallowed hard. 'What you mean is only a child would have been as stupid as to try and dislodge the ice tray with that old knife.'

'You said it! Anyway, let's examine the wound.' Solemnly he unwrapped her hand. 'Plaster quickly, Sister. Not very big but…that'll do,' he conceded as she plundered the first-aid kit beside the sink.

'Good as new.' He drew her to her feet. 'I'll send you my bill by return of post. Talking of which—a fee, that is—I've negotiated on your behalf that you'll get paid Sister's rates pro rata whenever you help us out at the hospital.'

Demelza's eyes widened. 'Really?'

'Of course. You're a professional. I wouldn't expect you to work for nothing. I pointed out to the powers that be that having an experienced sister on the island was a valuable asset. You reserve the right to accept only the medical assignments you choose, of course. We'll only ask you to work at the hospital if you're free and if we really need you. Would you accept this arrangement?'

'Well, put like that, of course I accept. I enjoyed working in hospital when Katia had her Caesarean. It's so good to be back in the saddle again.'

'Great to have you on board, Sister,' he said quietly. And then Nick bent his head and kissed her gently on the lips.

'Haven't got the contract for you to sign yet so I thought we should seal it with something a little more enjoyable,' he whispered huskily, as he pulled away. 'Please, don't be put off by my unprofessional manner.'

'Well, after all, we are off duty, Doctor,' she said lightly.

She recognised that she was actually flirting with Nick, and it was a long time since she'd indulged in that kind of behaviour. She smiled up at him and her heart turned over as she saw his response to her lighter mood.

'You're changing by the minute, Demelza,' he said.

When his lips came down on hers again she almost gasped at her own reaction. It was so difficult not to throw caution to the winds and simply allow her treacherous body to relax against Nick and give herself up to his enthralling embrace.

She leaned against him, revelling in the feel of his

hard, muscular body against hers. His hands moved to caress her, whilst his lips teased and tantalised her.

With an effort she pulled herself away. She was reaching the point of no return, the point at which she wanted, with every fibre of her being, to make love with Nick. But she was afraid to go along with the delicious desires that were sweeping over her.

She looked up into Nick's eyes and saw only tenderness.

'I'm sorry,' she whispered. 'It's been so long since—'

'Daddy! Daddy, I'm home!'

The small excited voice shrilled up to them from the courtyard. 'Katerina said you'd come home early so she let me come straight back to you. Where are you?'

Nick gave a resigned smile. 'I'm up here at Demelza's.'

'Great! Can I come up?'

Nick laughed as he heard the pounding of Ianni's feet on the stone steps. 'Sounds like you're up!'

Wordlessly, he took hold of Demelza's hand and pressed it to his lips. She held her breath. It was such a precious gesture to make. It signified that he understood. She took a deep breath as she followed him out into the bright sunshine. Maybe Nick thought he understood her reaction and now assumed that she was never going to let down her guard.

But never was a very long time. And she would have to revise her thinking if she was to put herself out of her emotional torment.

'Demelza!' Ianni rushed towards her, his arms outstretched.

She knelt down and hugged the excited boy. Looking up, she saw that Nick was watching them with a tender expression. For an instant she allowed herself the luxury of imagining what it would be like if she were Ianni's mother and Nick was…

'Can we go to Giorgio's this evening for supper, Daddy? All three of us. You, Demelza and—'

'I'm not sure what Demelza has planned for this evening, but if she's free…'

'I haven't got any plans for this evening so I'd love to come with you.' Demelza knew she was only adding to her involvement with Nick but it felt so right. It was as if she'd suddenly been planted in the middle of a ready-made family. And the warm feeling sweeping over her put paid to her fear of moving on into a more loving relationship…for the moment.

Later, when her skin had stopped tingling from the feel of Nick's caressing hands, she would be able to reassess the situation. But for tonight…

CHAPTER FIVE

DEMELZA was in her surgery early the next morning, even earlier than Irini who usually made a point of preparing everything before she arrived. It was very rare that she couldn't sleep, but last night had seemed impossibly long and tedious. The thoughts teeming through her mind had made it impossible to do anything other than lie still and try to relax her body.

At one point, she thought of the advice she'd given to Bryony—read a book. Well, she hadn't even attempted that remedy because her mind had been so crowded that she'd known she wouldn't have been able to concentrate.

She stood at the window now, looking out over the almost deserted beach. A young couple jogged past, taking advantage of the relative cool of the morning to get some exercise before the hot sun took away their good resolutions to get fit while on holiday. Seeing Demelza at the window, the young woman waved a hand.

Demelza waved back as she recognised her as a patient from yesterday's surgery. The young woman was called Fiona and she'd called in to ask about the best time of the month to get pregnant. Apparently, she and her partner, Tim, had been trying for a baby for six months, so far without success. They'd come out to Kopelos to see if a holiday would have any better result, because they'd both been leading very busy, stressful lives. They seemed to be a happy, well-suited pair and, from what she'd seen of them, Demelza felt they would make excellent parents.

Fiona had also asked Demelza about investigating the possibility of attending a fertility clinic back in England. Demelza had advised her patient to wait a few more months and see whether natural conception was possible. Six months wasn't very long to have tried for a baby and now that Fiona was working from home and not having to travel into work as a commuter every day, she might be more relaxed and mother nature would have more of a chance.

She went back to her desk, leaning against the back of the chair as she reviewed her own situation, and her confused thoughts about Nick came tumbling back. Last night at Giorgio's taverna, they'd had another great evening together. Having Ianni with them had meant that any feelings of embarrassment they might have had about their passionate embrace earlier in the evening hadn't been allowed to surface.

She'd been introduced to Nick's aunt this time. Anna had smiled and been very pleasant with her, but Demelza had felt she'd been sizing her up. Possibly wondering what her intentions were concerning Nick?

Well, what *were* her intentions? If she could answer that thousand-dollar question she wouldn't have to stay awake all night worrying!

Although Nick had been so loving towards her when they'd embraced yesterday afternoon, he'd probably just been carried away momentarily by the close rapport that had temporarily developed between them. It could have been a combination of the sun, their relaxed off-duty situation, some natural need to caress someone… She'd thought of any number of reasons that might have made Nick so passionate towards her. But as far as a relationship went, she mustn't read anything into it because Nick had said that after Lydia he didn't want any more complications in his life.

And then she remembered how she'd welcomed Nick's advances with open arms…literally! She'd been totally shameless before she'd pulled herself away. She thought of how she'd felt as if liquid fire were coursing through her veins…

'*Kali mera*, good morning, Sister Demelza. You're early today.'

Irini breezed in, her white uniform dress crisply ironed, her long dark hair pinned up on the top of her head and her young eager face smiling at Demelza as she took hold of one of the trolleys and began to wheel it outside to be checked and reset.

'There is a lady waiting already outside. I told her you didn't start your clinic as early as this but…'

'Send her in, Irini.'

Demelza fell into her professional mode. Work always took her mind off her own personal problems.

The woman's face was worried as she came in.

'I'm Josie Donaldson, Sister.'

'Demelza Tregarron.' Demelza put out her hand and clasped the other woman's, feeling that her patient needed to be put at her ease before they could begin any kind of consultation.

The woman's face brightened slightly as she sat down on a chair beside Demelza. 'I've heard that name before. Demelza. It's Cornish, isn't it?'

Demelza smiled. 'I was born in Cornwall.'

'My grandparents lived in Cornwall and I used to spend my long school holiday with them. All a long time ago. I'm nearly thirty-five.'

'Oh, you poor old thing,' Demelza said in a jocular

voice. 'I'll be thirty-five myself in three years. So, what can I do for you, Josie?'

Josie hesitated. 'I've been very stupid…'

'We all are at times. What happened?' Demelza waited for her patient to elaborate.

The woman gave a deep sigh. 'I met a bloke last night in the bar. We had a few drinks and then went back to his room. I don't normally do these things but when you're on holiday…I haven't had a holiday for years. Been looking after my mum, but she died last month and I thought, well, time's passing me by. I'll go on holiday. Try and snap out of it…'

Someone else escaping the past. Demelza waited until Josie decided to go on with the story. If she interrupted now her patient might clam up and leave. It was obviously difficult for her to continue.

Josie ran a hand through her short blonde hair. 'At first I was flattered. I've never had time to bother with men and it was great when he told me I was attractive. I know I'm not, but what with the alcohol and…well, to cut a long story short we went to bed. It's years since I did anything like that and I wasn't prepared. Neither was he…so we had unprotected sex…'

Josie began to cry. Demelza stood up and put an arm around the heaving shoulders. When the sobs began to diminish she sat down on her chair again.

'Are you going to see this man again?' she asked quietly.

Josie raised her sad eyes, runny with tears, and her mascara-streaked cheeks. Demelza handed her a tissue and her patient began to dab ineffectively at her face.

'I hope not! He told me he was married—after we'd had sex that is, the swine!'

'The oldest trick in the book,' Demelza said, in a

sympathetic tone. 'You wouldn't believe how many patients have told me a similar story. So now…?'

'So now I want to be absolutely sure I'm not pregnant. Have you got the morning-after pill out here?'

'Yes, we have,' Demelza said guardedly. 'But are you really sure about this? Taking emergency contraception pills, which are now widely known as the morning-after pill, can have side effects. I'll have to ask you a few questions about your health, Josie. There's rather a long list of other medical problems which would prevent me from prescribing ECP pills.'

As Demelza went through all the medical conditions that might cause side effects if the ECP pills were taken, she was pleased to find that Josie hadn't suffered from any of them. She looked across and smiled at her patient as she finished questioning her. 'Well, you seem to be in good health, Josie.'

'I've always made a point of looking after myself, going to the gym three times a week, swimming every other day, whatever I could fit in when I wasn't looking after Mum.'

Demelza had been relieved to find how well her surgery clinic was stocked when she first arrived. There was a good supply of ECPs. This was the first morning-after pill she'd been asked for and she was in no doubt that it wouldn't be the last. Holiday romances were often transitory affairs. But even with a healthy woman, there could be side effects and it was her duty to make Josie aware of this.

Her patient leaned forward, a pleading expression on her face. 'Please, Sister Demelza, can you give me a pill? And the sooner the better because I don't want to have anything more to do with that creep and I can't bear to think how stupid I've been and—'

'Josie, even though you appear to be healthy, you could still suffer side effects. About fifty per cent of women who take ECPs experience nausea and twenty per cent vomit. And if the patient vomits, there's a chance that her body won't absorb the pill and if a pregnancy has already started—'

'Please, Sister! I'll put up with anything so long as I'm going to do all I can to make sure I didn't get pregnant by that horrible man.'

'It's not a one hundred per cent remedy,' Demelza said.

Josie gave a big sigh. 'It's the only life line I can take...so, Sister, please...'

Demelza patted her patient's hand. 'Don't upset yourself, Josie. I had to make all these checks before I can even consider prescribing to you. I'm going to do everything I can for you.'

She stood up and went over to unlock her medical supplies cupboard to remove one of the packets. She opened it out and showed it to Josie.

'As you can see, there are two pills to take. They must be taken within seventy-two hours of unprotected sex, so we're OK on the timing. You can take the first one now.'

Demelza handed her patient a glass of water so that she could swallow it.

'You must take the second pill in exactly twelve hours so make a note of the time now and don't forget to take it.'

Josie smiled. 'Don't worry, Sister. I couldn't possibly forget.' She clutched her precious packet.

'If you suffer any side effects, come back to see me, Josie. And make sure you go to see your doctor back home in three to four weeks.'

Josie pulled a face. 'Do I have to?'

'I would strongly advise it. It's for your own good to make sure that you're still healthy. There is also the danger of sexually transmitted disease to think about.'

'I know! That's worrying me as well.'

'Go and have a check-up at a special clinic as soon as you get back to the UK. I've got a list here you can take with you. They're all very discreet and it would give you peace of mind.'

She handed over the printed list to her patient who ran her eyes over the page. 'I'll do that, Sister.'

Josie was standing up now. 'Thanks a lot. It said in the beach resort brochure that I'll have to pay for medicines at the clinic.'

Demelza gave her a slip of paper. 'Give that to Irini. She handles the finances. I hope you enjoy the rest of your holiday, Josie.'

Josie turned at the door and smiled. 'I'll try to. I won't make a fool of myself again, but it's so difficult when you're on your own and feeling lonely.'

Demelza smiled back. 'I'm sure it is,' she said sympathetically.

She leaned back in her chair after the patient had gone. Josie was going to try not to make a fool of herself again. She herself had almost cast all caution to the winds yesterday. She'd been within seconds of allowing her body to take over. Josie was right—it was hard when you were lonely. She herself wasn't lonely exactly, but she'd been on her own for so long that being with Nick had turned her head. She longed to be wanted, longed to feel his strong arms holding her against him until...

The ringing phone brought her back to the present. 'Sister Demelza here... Yes, Nick?'

She felt her pulses begin to race again and realised, with a pang, that Nick's telephone voice had the same effect on her as it did face to face. Pull yourself together, girl! You're on duty and it's probably only a professional query.

It was. Nick, in his most professional voice, was asking if she could help out at the hospital that afternoon.

'I want to do a hip replacement in Theatre this afternoon. Normally, I would send the patient to Athens or Rhodes, but it's an elderly lady who doesn't want to leave the island and if we don't do it here, she's refusing to have it done. If she doesn't have the hip replaced she'll be in a wheelchair for the rest of her life. I've had a look at your CV again and I see that you did some orthopaedic surgery during your time in London.'

Demelza smiled. 'Been checking up on me, have you?'

'Well, we really haven't got anybody else who would be so experienced here at the moment. Our orthopaedic sister is on maternity leave so if you wouldn't mind...?'

'What time?'

'Two o'clock. Ask Stavros to drive you up here.'

She grinned. 'How can I get Stavros to slow down?'

She heard the amusement in Nick's voice. 'You can't. He's genetically programmed to try and beat the sound barrier. Just fasten your seat belt and pray. That's what I do if ever I have to travel with him.'

'Thanks very much, Doctor.'

'My pleasure, Sister.'

Demelza arrived at the hospital half an hour early, needing to give herself recovery time from her whirl-

wind journey and time to become fully acquainted with
the theatre procedure for the hip replacement operation.

The nurse in Reception showed her along to Nick's
consulting room.

'Good! You're early. Do sit down, Demelza, while
I fill you in on the details of the case.'

It was very much business as usual, Demelza thought
as she sank down into a chair at the other side of Nick's
desk. A computer whirred quietly in one corner of the
small room. Medical textbooks completely lined one
wall. Nick's desk was littered with case notes and pa-
pers. Demelza wondered how he could appear so efficient with such a chaotic desk.

He ran a hand through his thick dark hair. She noticed it was slightly damp, as was his creased white
shirt, which had the sleeves rolled up above his elbows.
He'd probably been working hard all morning and now
was going to perform a hip replacement. She doubted
very much if he would have taken a break.

'Have you had lunch?' she asked quickly.

He raised an eyebrow and he grinned. 'Is that an
invitation?'

She blushed. 'No, no. I merely thought you looked
as if you'd been working all morning and—'

'Don't worry about me. I can keep going when I
have to. I've just had a sandwich and some coffee.
How about you?'

'I finished my clinic at twelve so I've had time for
a salad and some fruit.'

It felt strange to be discussing lunch with Nick in
this stilted way. There was no doubt in her mind that
he was feeling as uneasy about where their relationship
was heading as she was.

'So, fill me in on the details of this afternoon's case,'

she said, unnerved by the enigmatic expression in his eyes as he looked at her across the desk.

'Our patient is called Maria and she's seventy-two years old. She's known me since I was born so she tries to keep me in my place.'

Nick smiled. 'Maria is very stubborn and none of her family can get her to see sense. They thought I might be able to have some influence over her but I haven't.'

He broke off and pulled a wry face. 'As you've probably gathered, I'm very fond of her and I only want what's best for her. Anyway, her family and I have been trying to persuade Maria to go over to Athens to have her left hip replaced. She seemed to agree for a while, so I got her on the waiting list there.'

He leaned back in his chair and sighed. 'If only it had been that simple. As the date for the operation approached she dug in her heels and said she wasn't going. Her friend had been to Athens for an operation a few years ago and she'd died under the anaesthetic. I tried to explain to Maria that her friend's case had been entirely different but she wouldn't listen. All she would say was that if I wouldn't do the operation here then she was going to put up with the wheelchair her son had bought her.'

'So when did you decide to give in to Maria?'

'I've been in touch with the orthopaedic consultant in Athens every day for a week now, ever since Maria's son brought her into the hospital and asked if I could do something to persuade her to go to Athens. She was in terrible pain and he couldn't bear to see her suffer.'

'I don't remember meeting Maria when you showed me round the hospital, Nick. She sounds like the sort of feisty patient I would have remembered.'

'The nurse said Maria was taking her afternoon nap, so we didn't disturb her.' He smiled. 'You're right. You would have remembered her. I had hoped to be able to fly her over to Athens in the air ambulance this morning. Her orthopaedic consultant asked me to do all the usual pre-operative preparations—blood for grouping and cross-matching, and haemoglobin and electrolyte estimation. The hip area had been shaved and the skin prepared, but at the last minute, Maria refused to go, so I took charge and decided to operate here. The main problem was that my orthopaedic sister is on maternity leave. But with you here...'

Demelza nodded and Nick continued. 'I contacted Athens to advise them of the situation. A Charnley hip replacement prosthesis has just been flown in and we're ready to go.'

He jumped to his feet. 'So are you quite happy with all this? As you can see, we have a strange way of doing things out here.'

Demelza smiled, partly to hide the nervousness that was creeping over her. 'Well, you said it, Nick! I can't imagine a London hospital being quite so co-operative with the patient in a case like this, can you?'

'Absolutely not! But I can't stand by and see one of my oldest friends spend the rest of her life in a wheel-chair—even if she is a stubborn old so-and-so,' he finished with a wry grin.

Demelza scrubbed up beside Nick in the small ante-theatre. She'd already checked with the nurse on the instruments they were to use. It had been a long time since she'd assisted at a hip replacement operation but she found she hadn't forgotten the procedure.

A nurse fastened the back of Demelza's sterile gown and helped her to pull on the sterile gloves. Following

Nick into Theatre, some of her earlier nervousness returned. But one glance at his steady, earnest eyes across the operating table and she felt her confidence flooding back. Her hands were steady as she handed him a scalpel to make the first incision.

As Nick exposed the head of the femur, Demelza could see that the diseased bone had almost crumbled away to nothing.

'Now you can see why I felt this operation was urgent, Sister,' he said.

She nodded. 'I can see why you're having to do a total hip replacement.'

Nick looked up briefly to speak to the two nurses assisting Demelza. 'I'm going to remove the diseased part of the bone and insert the prosthesis down into the femur.'

He then explained how he would fix the head of the prosthesis into the acetabulum in the bone of the pelvis.

Demelza found herself admiring the calm way in which Nick worked, patiently explaining what he was doing at every step of the way. Before she'd realised it the operation was finished and the patient was ready to be wheeled back to the ward.

Nick gave final instructions to the two nurses who were going to give special round-the-clock nursing care to Maria.

As she pulled off her gloves and tossed them in the bin, Demelza turned to Nick and remarked that it hadn't been very different to working in a London operating theatre.

'The air-conditioning helps,' Nick said. 'Otherwise…'

'I wasn't talking about the air-conditioning,'

Demelza said. 'I was impressed that we were able to do the operation with so few staff and so little fuss.'

Nick pulled off his theatre cap and looked down at her. Demelza noticed that his unruly hair was even more ruffled. It made him look so boyish and so...yes, dared she admit it? So desirable...

He put a finger under her chin and tilted her face so that she had to look up into his eyes. 'I'm glad you approve of the methods in our little hospital because I entirely approve of the way you handled a difficult situation. I didn't tell you before the operation, but if Maria had had to wait much longer it would have been too late for the operation to be successful.'

'I could see that by the state of her femur,' she said, wondering when Nick was going to move from this deliciously close position.

He moved his finger upwards and touched her cheek. She remained absolutely still, feeling mesmerised by the tantalisingly tender expression in his eyes. And then, as she'd hoped, he bent his head and kissed her, oh, so gently on the lips. She heard a gasp, and realised it was herself. She'd been waiting for the touch of his lips, longing for some form of physical contact with him.

The swing door flew open and Demelza jumped back.

'Dr Capodistrias...oh, sorry, sir. I didn't know you were...er, busy. I wondered if I could have a word with you about Maria.'

Demelza felt sorry for the hapless nurse who'd just barged in. Sorry and guilty that once again she'd cast aside all caution. She'd been positively angling for Nick's attentions ever since the operation had finished and been declared successful.

Nick was totally in command of the situation. 'Of course, Nurse. What's the problem?'

Demelza moved towards the door. Her brief had been to assist at the operation so she wouldn't interfere in the after-care of the patient.

'Just a moment, Sister.'

Nick's studiously professional tone brought her to a halt.

'If you'd like to wait for me I'll give you a lift back to the village. You could call Stavros if you prefer,' he added dryly.

Demelza smiled. 'Thank you very much, Dr Capodistrias. I accept your kind offer.'

She wished she was still wearing her theatre mask as she felt the annoying blush spreading over her cheeks. But if she'd been wearing a mask she wouldn't have experienced Nick's tantalising kiss.

She waited in the staff common room. It was a small room littered with medical magazines and empty coffee-cups. Typical of all the hospital common rooms she'd ever been in except that it had the most mind-blowing view of the bay. She was so entranced with the view as she stood at the window that she didn't hear Nick arrive through the open door and come up behind her.

She jumped as she felt a hand on her shoulder.

'Sorry! I didn't mean to startle you.'

'You didn't!'

She turned and felt again a mixture of embarrassment and desire as she looked up at Nick. Her lips were still tingling from the touch of his kiss and her body was in a state of heightened awareness. 'I...I was just admiring the view of the harbour.'

Nick's hand was still lightly resting on her shoulder,

a comforting, soothing, sympathetic touch. She tried to tell herself that their relationship was based purely on the mutual understanding they had of each other's problems but she failed to convince herself. She longed for more than mere sympathy from this exciting man. And from the kisses they'd exchanged she couldn't help hoping that he was beginning to feel the same way.

She looked down at the harbour, the bright blue water glistening in the late afternoon sunlight as she tried to become accustomed to the feel of Nick's hand on her shoulder. It was no good telling herself it was a friendly gesture. It was more than that—to her at least.

Down below in the harbour, the inter-island ferry was just leaving after the fascinating bustle of the loading of cargo—sheep, goats, hens and people—and the unloading of fruit and vegetables had been completed. Smartly dressed people from a cruise ship and casually dressed people from the various yachts which had tied up during the day were beginning to drift along the harbourside in search of the best taverna for an evening out.

Suddenly, the excitement of the impending evening began to get to her. She'd never been one to go out on the town—as her mother-in-law had disparagingly referred to an evening out—but she suddenly felt she wanted to do something different. And the longings that Nick was constantly stirring up in her were giving her ideas. The bright lights weren't her scene. She was more into a cosy night in with someone she felt at ease with.

She turned round, looking up into Nick's eyes. 'Would you and Ianni like to have supper at my place tonight? I'd like to cook something for all of us.'

Nick looked surprised. 'Great! How could I possibly turn down an offer like that? You're sure?'

'Just simple home cooking,' she said quickly.

'Mmm, sounds good to me. I love Greek cooking but sometimes I long for a change.'

'Shepherd's pie?' she said, planning to play safe with one of her tried and tested remedies.

Nick grinned. 'How did you guess that's one of my favourites? My English grandmother used to make that for me.'

Oh, well, if Nick's grandmother used to make it, he couldn't read anything into this evening other than a friendly invitation meant to repay some of the meals she'd enjoyed with him at the taverna.

Nick parked his Land Rover at the end of the village street that led to the villa. There was only room for a donkey to walk down the street. In the early days when motorbikes had first arrived on the island, the young men of the village had zoomed down between the ancient houses. But a petition from the villagers had convinced the mayor that motorbikes must be banned on narrow streets.

Ianni gave a whoop of excitement when he saw Nick and Demelza walking towards where he was playing outside Katerina's house with Lefteris.

'Daddy! Demelza!' The little boy flung himself against his father for a hug.

Then it was Demelza's turn. Her heart was full of happiness as she hugged the excited boy. The feeling of belonging was almost too much for her. She'd hoped for a new life when she'd come out here but hadn't dared to find herself accepted into a family.

Careful, she told herself as the three of them walked

the remaining stretch of the street to the villa. Don't take too much for granted. Don't try to take over as mother. You're simply a friend, regardless of the deep maternal instincts that Ianni is stirring up.

'I've got to stop off at the shop,' she said, pausing outside the fascinating little house crammed to the ceiling with every conceivable kind of goods, whilst fruit and vegetable boxes sprawled out into the street.

'Can I come in with you, Demelza?' Ianni asked. 'I've still got some spending money left for sweets.'

Demelza glanced at Nick. He was grinning as he nodded. 'Not too many, Ianni. We're going out for supper, remember?'

Demelza bought everything she would need for the meal—minced lamb, herbs, potatoes, onions—while Nick supervised the all-important choosing of the sweets. She'd bought the basics for her food cupboard and fridge already.

Nick was very firm with Ianni when they reached the villa and insisted that he do his homework and change out of his school uniform before they went up to Demelza's apartment for supper.

'See you both later,' she said, as she ran up the steps to her apartment.

She hadn't felt so excited about making a meal in a long time! That's all it was, a simple meal. But it meant so much more to her to know that she was going to spend the evening with Nick in a safe situation where she didn't have to worry about where their relationship was going.

CHAPTER SIX

STANDING at the cooker, stirring the mince into the fried onions, Demelza could see the relaxed evening stretching ahead of her. Nick and Ianni would be coming up to join her soon. It would be just the three of them round the table and…

Suddenly she put down her spoon at the side of the cooker and pulled the pan off the heat. What was she doing, planning to set up a cosy little family unit? Would Nick feel as if she was trying to take over his personal life? He'd told her that there were too many complications in his life already. But she wasn't planning to be a further complication. Just someone who was very close to him, mentally and physically. Whenever they were close together, she could feel a strong magnetic pull that told her they were so right for each other, so…

'Daddy's in the shower,' said a small voice.

Demelza turned and saw Ianni outlined in the doorway, with the rays of the setting sun behind him. His hair was still wet from the shower, his feet were bare and he was wearing white cotton pyjamas. He looked like a little cherub.

'Can I come in, Demelza?' he said.

'Of course you can.'

She walked across to meet him and he put his little hand in hers.

'I've got my jimjams on,' Ianni said solemnly. 'Daddy said I could wear what I liked, so I thought I'd get into my jimjams so I don't have to do any more undressing and dressing. It's such a pain, isn't it?'

Demelza nodded. 'I've put this dress on because it's nice and cool for cooking in.'

'It's very pretty,' Ianni said, fingering the lime green cotton. He looked up at her. 'It sort of goes with your hair. Your hair is pretty, too. Can I touch it?'

She bent down so that Ianni could take a strand between his thumb and finger. 'What do you think, Ianni?'

'Did you have to make it this colour with some stuff from a bottle, Demelza?'

Demelza laughed. 'No, it was this colour when I was born, but I think it's faded a bit.'

'My mum's hair must have faded a lot because she has to keep putting blonde stuff on it. I asked her what colour it really was and she said she couldn't remember and I shouldn't be so nosy.'

'Does Daddy know you've come up here, Ianni?'

'Well…er…'

'No, Daddy doesn't know!' Nick bent his head to come in through the doorway, which hadn't been made for tall people. 'You scalliwag! Demelza needs a bit of peace and quiet so she can get on with the cooking.'

'That's OK,' Demelza said quickly. 'Ianni can help me.'

'Ooh, yes, please! What can I do?'

'You can mash these cooked potatoes and make them nice and soft. Here…let's put some butter on them… That's fine… Press as hard as you like. You can't spoil them…'

Demelza turned away from the table where Ianni was now crouching on a chair, bashing on the potatoes with a wide, happy smile on his face. Nick was standing close behind her, a tender expression in his eyes. Like his son's, his hair was still wet from the shower and he looked as if he'd thrown on the chinos and shirt very quickly because there was only one shirt button done up above his belt. The sight of his dark chest made her pulses race.

'I've never done any cooking before,' Ianni said, pounding away at the potatoes. 'Mum always says I get in the way in the kitchen. Anyway, she doesn't do much cooking.'

Nick's eyes flickered. 'Ianni, I had a letter from Mum today. She's decided she can come out to stay in July.'

Ianni continued to work on the potatoes, making no sign that he'd even heard his father.

But Demelza could see from the way he pursed his lips that he was weighing up the idea. She moved back towards the table.

'I think that's perfect now, Ianni,' she said. 'We'll spread the potatoes over the meat…like this…and then we'll put them in the oven…like so… Mind your fingers…'

She was trying to work out why Ianni's natural exuberance had suddenly diminished. He'd made no comment on the fact that his mother was coming out in July.

'It will be nice having Mummy here, won't it?' she asked lightly.

'Yes,' Ianni said, in a flat voice.

Demelza glanced at Nick. His expression was giving nothing away. She wouldn't try to probe. It was obvious there was some kind of problem with the mother-and-son relationship but that would probably sort itself out when they spent time together out here. Why else would Lydia be coming out except to be with her son? From what Nick had told her it had been an acrimonious divorce so she couldn't be coming to see Nick...or could she?

Was Lydia still holding a candle for her ex-husband? Demelza studiously avoided that line of thought.

'Let's all have a drink,' she said brightly. 'We can take our glasses out on the terrace and watch the sunset over the hills. There's a bottle of wine in the fridge, Nick, if you'd like to open it, and I've got lemonade for Ianni.'

They all sat out on the terrace, Ianni happily munching his way through a packet of crisps before helping Demelza and Nick to eat the olives.

'I keep meaning to find out how I can get my shower put right, Nick. Do you know who owns my apartment?'

Nick smiled. 'I most certainly do. You're looking at him.'

'Oh...I'm sorry! I'd no idea.'

'The villa belonged to my family. When my father died and my mother and I went to live in England, my grandparents looked after it. I used to come out to see them whenever I could. After they died I was totally responsible for the place even though my relatives used to keep an eye on it for me. After I'd decided to come and live out here, I got a builder in to deal with the major repairs and turn this top storey into a self-contained flat. The rent from the flat, which is paid direct to me by the travel company, helps to pay for the repairs and rebuilding. What is the problem with the shower?'

Demelza swallowed hard. Nick had been so positive when he'd talked about his father dying and he and his mother having to move back to England. But she could tell that it had been a traumatic time for him. And here she was worrying about her shower!

'It's only a simple thing,' she said quickly. 'I just can't get used to using a hand shower and—'

Nick clapped a hand to his forehead. 'I'm so sorry! That was one of the things I meant to have done before you came, but it completely slipped my mind. You're the first person in here. I'll speak to the plumber to-morrow.'

'Thanks.' She hesitated. 'It must have been a great relief for you to come back to Kopelos, having been born here.'

Ianni had already got down from his chair to play with a pile of small stones in the corner of the terrace which the builders had left behind. Nick didn't seem to be worried about the state of Ianni's pyjamas and Ianni was happy with the house he was building so it seemed a pity to stop him. There was nothing that a bit of soap and water wouldn't put right.

Nick leaned back in his chair. 'It felt like I was home at last,' he said, his voice husky with emotion. 'My father was born out here. Like my grandfather, he was a fisherman so he was, of course, an expert sailor. Which was why I couldn't believe it when I found out that Dad had drowned at sea.'

Demelza leaned forward. 'Do you know what happened?' she asked softly.

Nick took a deep breath. 'A big storm blew up quickly after the fishing fleet had gone out. Normally, they have warning of bad weather approaching but that day the storm arrived before anyone was prepared. Five sailors were drowned, my father among them. At first they didn't tell me why Dad hadn't come back. But at the age of six…'

Nick glanced across at his son. 'Ianni's age. You're not stupid, especially when everybody around you is crying or… Anyway, my grandmother thought it would be better if I knew everything because she said I had to take care of my mother now that Dad was gone. Especially as my mother was expecting her second child. Mum had already told me why her tummy was getting bigger, I remember, and I was looking forward to having a playmate.'

He broke off and took a large gulp of wine. 'Anyway, Mum was homesick for England and her pregnancy wasn't going very well. We didn't have a hospital on the island in those days and my father's relatives worried about her. So Mum took me back to England and we stayed with my English grandparents. Three months later she went into hospital. The baby was stillborn and Mum died of eclampsia.'

Demelza could feel the tears pricking her eyes. Looking across at Nick, she could see that he'd come to terms with the tragedy but the deep scars were still inside him. That was the thing about suffering. You could get over it to a certain extent but it was always with you, buried deep, influencing the way you behaved and thought.

She leaned across the table and put her fingers on Nick's large hand. It was only a gesture of sympathy. He looked at her and she stood up and went round to put her hands on his shoulders. Slowly, he pulled himself to his feet and took her into his arms, holding her against him. She felt the warmth and strength of his body and it felt so right to be here in Nick's embrace.

And in that moment she knew she wanted to move things on. She wasn't going to hold back any more.

Both she and Nick had suffered, but life was too short to dwell on the past. Whatever kind of relationship developed, she was going to go for it. Nick's complicated background would make him wary of her intentions but she would make it quite clear that she didn't want to make any demands on him.

She pulled herself gently away from the circle of Nick's arms and looked across at Ianni. He was still totally absorbed in what he was doing. She smiled up at Nick.

'I think I'd better check on Ianni's grubby hands because supper's nearly ready.'

Nick reached out and touched her face, gently. 'I'll do that.'

'OK.' She moved quickly inside.

As she put the spinach in the pan she glanced out of the window. Nick was lifting Ianni up onto his shoulder, carrying him towards the door. She felt a surge of affection for both of them. Affection for Ianni, but a powerful love for Nick. Yes, she'd fallen in love, and her whole body felt alive again. The most she could hope for would be that Nick, given all the complications in his life, would be fond of her. That would do for the time being.

One day at a time. She would live for the moment.

The shepherd's pie was delicious, the spinach perfectly undercooked. She served fresh apricots as a dessert, but Ianni was already slumped against the back of his chair. Although his eyes were closing, he was still desperately trying to stay awake.

Nick got up from the table and carried him across

to the sofa, putting a couple of cushions under his head to make him comfortable.

'Let's have our coffee outside on the terrace,' Demelza whispered. 'It's cooler out there.'

He waited until she'd made the coffee in the cafetière then he carried the tray outside and placed it on the table. Demelza stacked the dishes in the sink before going out to join Nick on the terrace. In the moonlight she saw him rising from the table and coming towards her. His arms were outstretched and she moved into them as if it was the most natural thing in the world.

He held her against him, her head against his shoulder. When she raised her eyes she saw that he was looking down at her with that tender expression in his eyes that made her feel she was turning into liquid desire. He bent his head and kissed her on the mouth. She savoured the touch of his lips. She sighed as his kiss deepened and her body awakened to the touch of his caressing hands. She pressed herself against him and felt the sensual excitement as she recognised the hardening of his desire.

An unwelcome, ringing phone was making itself heard in her consciousness. Nick was cursing softly as he reached for his mobile. She moved out of the circle of his arms and sat down at the table. Reaching for the cafetière, she poured out a couple of cups, black and strong. She needed something to bring her back to earth. She could hear Nick talking in rapid Greek, and from his earnest face she deduced it was the hospital.

'I gather you're on call,' she said, as he broke the connection and sat down beside her at the table.

She handed him a coffee-cup. He took a sip before explaining.

'Technically, I'm always on call. You see, I'm in

charge of the running of the hospital as well as working as a hands-on doctor there. I've got a good staff but they know they can always call me when it's something they can't sort out themselves.'

'So what's the problem?' Demelza had come back to earth again. Her body was still vibrant from the contact with Nick but the moment had passed. She was in control of her senses again and it looked as if Nick was already planning what to do about some medical emergency.

'It's Maria, our hip replacement. She's in a distressed state and convinced the operation was a disaster. She's saying that she wants to see me to ask me what I did with her leg. The night staff say she's very confused.'

Demelza gave a wry smile. 'So you're going to go and help them out?'

He nodded. 'I think I should. As far as I can gather, there are no real post-operative complications but I'd like to see for myself what's happening. I don't know how long I'll be but—'

'Don't worry about Ianni. I'll keep him here all night. He'll be quite safe on the sofa and it would be a shame to waken him.'

'I usually take him round to Katerina's if I'm called out at night.'

Demelza shook her head. 'Leave him here, Nick. I'll send him down in the morning.'

'You're very kind.'

Kind! That was the last thing she was feeling. Frustrated was more like it! Having made the momentous decision that she wouldn't let anything stand in her way, she would now have to wait for another time to make it obvious to Nick that she wanted to make love with him.

But that was what it was like in the medical profession. Patients always came first and personal relationships had to be put on the back burner.

He kissed her lightly on the cheek and hurried away down into the courtyard. She was sipping her coffee as she heard the clang of the courtyard door. Nick's footsteps echoed eerily down the deserted street.

As Nick climbed up into his Land Rover and started the engine he was feeling uneasy—and not just about the state of his patient. If the phone hadn't rung just now, would he have been able to stop himself from making love to Demelza? He took a deep breath to calm himself as he drove away from the village and headed towards the town.

Just holding Demelza's vibrant body in his arms had driven him wild with desire. He wanted her, oh, yes, he wanted her! He shifted in his seat as his desire made itself painfully obvious. He hadn't planned to make love with her tonight but whenever he allowed himself to kiss her he felt compelled to follow his natural instincts.

And he mustn't. He banged one hand down hard on the steering-wheel. He mustn't—well, at least not just yet! Demelza seemed so scared of becoming involved with him, which was perfectly natural for someone who'd been through a bad patch and forgotten what it was like to form a new relationship. She'd only just come out of the cloistered world of demanding relatives and she was terribly vulnerable. He mustn't confuse the way she'd clung to him as being a sign that she wanted to make love. He would have to restrain himself before he took things too far, because he couldn't bear to hurt her. She was like a delicate flower which would be crushed so easily by the wrong person.

But it would be so hard to control himself when he was close to her! Just remembering her soft hair against his face as he'd kissed her, the curves of her slim figure against him…

He gave himself a shake as he drove into the hospital car park. Time to pull himself together and concentrate on his patient!

Demelza leaned back in her chair and looked up at the moon. Perhaps it's best that I didn't go overboard tonight, she told herself. She hadn't known Nick very long. Maybe she would have been rushing things to have given herself completely tonight and perhaps she would have regretted it.

She doubted it! It had been obvious that Nick had wanted to make love. His embrace had been ardent, every fibre of his body seeming to demand fulfilment. But would he have held off because he thought it was too soon?

She shivered and her body tingled as the memories flooded through her. Quickly, she put the cups on the tray and went inside. Ianni was sleeping peacefully, one arm flung behind his head, his lips in a contented curve as if he was having a happy dream.

She pulled the cotton cover over him. It was warm but it would become a little cooler in the middle of the night. Leaving a small lamp lit in the corner of the room, she went through into her bedroom. She opened the door wide so that she would hear if Ianni woke up and became confused about his surroundings. Pulling off her clothes and putting on a large, thin cotton

T-shirt, she lay down beneath the flimsy sheet and closed her eyes.

Closing her eyes, Nick's handsome face appeared in her mind's eye again and it was a long time before she dozed off into a fitful sleep.

She was awakened by Ianni jumping onto her bed.

'Where's Daddy?'

Demelza smiled. 'He had to go to the hospital last night. I think he'll be back downstairs by now but we'd better check. Would you like to have some breakfast first?'

'Oh, yes, please!'

She climbed out of bed and pulled on her cotton housecoat. Ianni waited for her before putting his little hand in hers. Together they carried the breakfast things out onto the terrace. Demelza stretched her arms in the air and took a deep breath. It was the sort of morning that made you feel good to be alive. The sun, already warm, was climbing higher over the sea down there beyond the red rooftops of the village.

It was quiet down below in Nick's apartment. She would investigate after they'd had breakfast. Either Nick was still at the hospital or else he was trying to catch up on his sleep. And she was enjoying having Ianni with her for breakfast.

She spread some butter and honey on his toast and handed it to him on a plate. He chewed noisily, showing his enjoyment.

'I love honey, Demelza,' the little boy said, between bites. 'The bees make it up there on the hillside but they don't like you watching them. Lefteris got stung once and Katerina was cross with him. I think she should have been cross with the bees, don't you? We were only having a look at them. We didn't mean to harm them. I can't think why bees can be so horrid and still make lovely honey like this. Can I have some more, please?'

Demelza smiled. 'Of course.'

She heard the door of Nick's apartment opening as she was spreading Ianni's next slice of toast. Leaning over the terrace wall, she saw him coming out, rubbing his eyes sleepily. He was barefoot, wearing only a pair of shorts and looking desirably sexy.

'Good morning, Nick.'

'Oh, hi!'

'Daddy, we're up here having breakfast. There's some scrummy honey. Come on up! Oh, you don't mind, do you, Demelza?' the little boy asked as an afterthought.

Demelza laughed. 'Of course I don't mind if Daddy would like to have breakfast with us.'

'Just coffee please,' Nick said, bounding up the stairs. He sank down at the table. 'Are you all right, Demelza? I mean, you hadn't bargained for...for everything that happened when you invited us for supper last night.'

His dark eyes held an enigmatic expression as he looked across at her. She knew he was remembering their passionate embrace, probably wondering if she was regretting it.

'I'm fine. I'm enjoying myself,' she said quietly.

'Good!' He reached and took hold of her hand. 'Because I enjoyed myself last night and I wouldn't want anything to spoil—'

'Dad, did I tell you that Lefteris got stung by a bee last week?'

Nick gave a wry grin. 'No, you didn't. What happened?'

'Well, we were just up there on the hill and there was this gate, so Lefteris untied the piece of rope round it so we could go in and look at the bees' houses—they're called beehives—and...'

Demelza got up from the table to go inside and make some more coffee. Ianni was still chattering when she returned.

'Just a minute, Ianni,' Nick said, breaking into the flow. 'I need to tell Demelza something about the patient I had to see in hospital last night.'

'Yes, I wanted to ask you how Maria was,' Demelza said.

'She's fine, as far as the operation is concerned. It's always a difficult time, as you know, in the first few post-operative days, but she was scared by being in hospital and simply wanted me to hold her hand, I think.'

Demelza knew the feeling! She was sure that Nick's bedside manner would be very much sought after by his patients.

Nick put down his coffee. 'I checked out the site of the prosthesis—the wound is clean. No problems there. The physiotherapist is coming in today to start post-operative exercises and as soon as we can we'll get Maria out of bed and moving around. That's not going to be easy because Maria thinks she's just going to lie comfortably there and her mobility will return as if by magic.'

Demelza smiled. 'I've known a few patients like that.'

Nick stood up. 'I've got to get moving, Demelza.'

'Me, too,' Demelza said, as she began to clear the

things from the table. 'Irini will probably be beavering away already, preparing for the morning surgery.'

'How do you find Irini?'

'She's excellent, thoroughly reliable.'

Nick smiled. 'Good. I handpicked her myself. She's related to Giorgio at the taverna, and so related by marriage to my father's family.'

'You seem to know everybody on the island.'

'It's a very close community which is one of the attractions of the place, at least for those of us who were born here. Katerina, who looks after Ianni when I'm not here, is my cousin. When we were very small we used to play together. She offered to look after Ianni for me and at first she wouldn't take any payment. But I persuaded her that I couldn't do my professional work without her so she ought to get paid like I did.'

'The people here are so warm-hearted. I haven't met anybody I dislike…but, then, I've only been here a few days.'

'It seems much longer,' Nick said.

'Yes.' She looked up and saw that wonderfully tender look in his eyes again.

Nick was obviously warming towards her but she doubted whether he was falling in love as she was. It was all too soon for him and maybe he wouldn't want to become too involved with someone who might prove to be a further complication in his life.

Demelza turned away and began carrying the plates and cups to the kitchen. Nick picked up the empty cafetière and followed her. She leaned over the sink and began swishing water around the plates.

'Thanks a lot…for everything,' Nick said.

She felt his hands lightly touching her shoulders but she didn't turn round.

'I enjoyed having Ianni here,' she said carefully.

She felt his hands gripping her shoulders and she turned to meet his gaze. He bent his head and kissed her lightly on the lips. She savoured the moment which ended all too quickly as he turned and strode away, as if kissing her had been the last thing on his mind.

Resuming the dishes, she wondered just how long she could contain her frustration. It was a good thing she had a busy morning ahead of her to take her mind off Nick!

CHAPTER SEVEN

DEMELZA switched off her computer as soon as she'd finished filing away the details of the patients she'd treated that morning. It had been a quiet surgery. She'd noticed that as the summer progressed the number of patients diminished. It was as if the now intense heat had cleared up all the coughs and colds, and most of the tourists wanted to get out on the beach and into the sea. Reporting minor ailments was the last thing on their minds. They were here to enjoy themselves in the sun, not worry about their health.

Looking out of the window now, she could see them all stretched out on their sunbeds, already soporific from the heat of the sun. Most of them were sensibly shaded by their umbrellas. She actually gave a short talk to each tour group as they arrived, telling them of the dangers of too much exposure to the sun's rays. Some of her instructions seemed to have sunk in. That was a relief! Back in May, her cases of sunburn had been bad enough, but now they'd reached July the sun was positively dangerous.

In her introductory talks she also stressed the importance of drinking bottled water, which seemed to have paid off, judging by the infrequency of gastric upsets.

July! Where had the weeks gone to? And why hadn't her relationship with Nick progressed any further when they spent so much time together? Apart from that first idyllic picnic on the deserted beach soon after she'd arrived here, there hadn't been anything remotely like a date together.

But the most frustrating thing was that Nick continued to take her in his arms sometimes, still looked at her with that tender expression that drove her wild with longing for him. But that was as far as it went!

She frowned as she got up and paced the room. The trouble was she was so naïve where love affairs were concerned. She didn't know the first thing about how to signal to a man that you wanted him! And Nick was an unknown quantity. He was Greek for a start—well, half-Greek—so it was more difficult to know how his mind worked. If she were to make it more obvious that she wanted to move their relationship on, would she scare him away? He'd said his life was complicated so maybe he was scared of becoming more involved with her.

She leaned against the window, staring out at the stretch of sand leading down to the brilliant blue sea as she realised that she couldn't change her nature. She'd had a sheltered upbringing with her caring but very strict, domineering parents. And she'd moved from being under their wing to committing herself entirely to Simon. So there'd never been any time when she'd experienced relationships with other men. It was incredible that at the ripe old age of thirty-two she should be so inexperienced! Incredible and frightening.

Demelza sighed heavily as she mused on the fact that all around her women were making the first move towards their men, but she wouldn't know how to begin!

Nick had made it obvious that he found her attractive. But was that as far as it went? Was he perfectly happy to go on as they were doing—meeting, sharing the occasional meal, stealing a kiss here and there, working together at the hospital sometimes and—?

Loud, excited voices coming from the waiting room broke in on her thoughts. Her door opened and Irini came in, looking anxious.

'We've got a very ill little girl, Sister. Will you have a look at her?'

'Of course. Bring her in.'

A distraught man was already coming through the door carrying a little girl of about five.

'I don't know what's wrong with my Sarah, Sister. She'd just started to eat her picnic out there under the umbrella when she started screaming that she couldn't swallow. But now she's gone all quiet and—'

'Let's get Sarah on the couch here,' Demelza said quickly. 'What was she eating when she started being ill?'

'We'd bought some bread rolls up in the village. Look, this is the one she was eating when—'

'Ah, sesame seeds!' Demelza said, taking hold of the half-eaten roll. 'Is Sarah allergic to sesame seeds?'

The man shook his head. 'Not that I know of. Well, as far as I know, she's never had any before. She's allergic to nuts and she had a bad reaction to a halva bar once. Her throat closed up and we had to take her to the hospital for treatment.'

'Halva is ground-up sesame seeds,' Demelza said, as she peered into her young patient's mouth.

She could see that the throat was swelling and closing up rapidly.

'Sarah's having an anaphylactic reaction to the sesame seeds,' she said evenly as she went over to the medicine cupboard. 'I'm going to give her a shot of adrenaline and some antihistamine medication. We'll have to watch her very carefully for the next few hours so I'm going to take her into hospital.'

Demelza was preparing the injection of adrenaline as she spoke. She glanced over her shoulder. 'Irini, will you phone the hospital and tell them I'm bringing in an emergency patient with an anaphylactic reaction to sesame seeds?'

It took only minutes to reach the hospital. On this occasion, Demelza was relieved that Stavros was the speediest driver on the island. Nick was waiting for them in the accident and emergency area.

He leaned over the little girl. 'Can you hear me, Sarah?'

The little girl moaned and opened her eyes. She gave a little cough, appearing for one anxious moment as if she was going to choke on her own saliva, and then, miraculously, she swallowed.

Demelza quickly filled Nick in on the details of the case—the state of the patient on arrival at the surgery and the adrenaline and antihistamine she'd already administered.

Nick nodded. 'The adrenaline's already had an effect. I'll just examine Sarah's throat.' He took a laryingoscope and peered down the little girl's throat.

When he straightened up he was smiling. 'Take a look, Sister.'

Demelza leaned over her young patient and the light on the laryingoscope lit up the throat.

'Excellent!' she breathed. 'What a relief! When I tried to examine Sarah's throat at the clinic, I couldn't see beyond the mouth.'

'Your daughter's going to be OK now,' Nick told

the father, whose hands were trembling nervously as he held onto little Sarah.

'Good girl!' the man whispered with relief as he stroked Sarah's soft fair hair. 'Mummy will be so relieved when I take you back.'

'I'd like to keep Sarah here for twenty-four hours,' Nick said quickly. 'Until we've made sure there are no further complications. The adrenaline and antihistamine Sister gave her have reduced the swelling but we need to do a full examination to see there are no further complications.'

The man nodded. 'Can I stay with her?'

Nick patted the worried father on the shoulder. 'Of course you can. I'll take you up to the children's ward as soon as I've checked Sarah over.'

Nick turned to look at Demelza. 'Thanks, Sister.'

There was a finality about his tone. She was being dismissed. He was anxious to get on with his work and she was no longer required.

She always experienced a sense of anticlimax when she left the hospital. This was where the action was. This was where real nursing was required and she realised that she would love to be on the permanent staff here. The beach resort clinic was on the periphery, though very necessary. But she'd been trained as a hospital nurse and at some point in the future she knew she would have to take on a more exacting role in her nursing career.

And the hospital was where Nick spent most of his time. He was totally dedicated to his patients and when she was working with him she felt the rapport growing between them. They worked well together. Neither of them ever mentioned this, but it was a growing professional bond that she valued.

It was a pity that their personal relationship seemed to be at a standstill!

Stavros was waiting for her when she went out into the hot midday sun. He smiled and opened the passenger door for her.

'Back to the beach, Sister?'

She smiled back. 'Yes, please.'

A couple of hours under a shady umbrella would help her to relax, and it would take her mind off Nick.

Demelza clambered over the rocks and found a quiet spot in the little bay around the corner from the main beach. A few couples were nearby but they weren't in the least bit interested in her. She could relax and have a restful afternoon. Stripping off to her bikini, she pulled out the bread rolls and feta cheese she'd bought in the village and ate her lunch.

Closing her eyes, she found herself drifting off to sleep…

A man's voice was speaking to her. Was she dreaming? She opened her eyes and stared in surprise.

'Nick! What are you doing here?' She sat up, rubbing her eyes as she tried to think straight.

He looked so out of place on the beach in his workday suit.

He smiled down at her. 'Stavros told me you were here. I'm supposed to be meeting Lydia but she hasn't arrived from the airport yet.'

'Lydia's coming today? You didn't tell me!'

As soon as she'd voiced her surprise and alarm, she wished she hadn't. It sounded as if she was interested in his relationship with his ex-wife, and there was nothing further from the truth!

Nick shrugged. 'Completely slipped my mind until Katerina reminded me this morning.'

Demelza stood up so that she didn't have to crane her neck to look at Nick. Grabbing her sarong, she tied it over her bikini, but not before she'd seen Nick's eyes lingering on her bare skin. She felt a surge of longing running through her. She wanted this man so much it almost hurt her to play the platonic friend.

Nick turned and pointed up the hill to where the road meandered its way down to the beach. 'I think that's the resort minibus arriving now. Will you come and meet Lydia with me?'

Demelza hesitated. 'Is that a good idea?'

Nick's eyes widened with surprise. 'Why not?'

She swallowed hard. This was another indication that she was merely a good friend. He wouldn't be introducing her to his ex-wife if they were more than friends, would he?

'Come on, Demelza. I can't stay long with her because I want to get back for Ianni.'

'In that case, I'll pack up here and you can give me a lift back, if that's OK.'

'Of course!' He picked up her bag.

'I ought to throw my clothes back on.'

'No time! The minibus is nearly here. You look great as you are. You can put your clothes on in the car.'

Demelza hurried after Nick, who was carrying everything for her. Her bare feet felt as if they were burning on the scorching hot sand. They reached the main building just as the minibus was pulling into the loading bay in front of Reception.

She felt like a peasant in her sarong and bare feet as Nick surged forward through the crowd around the bus.

He was still holding her bag so she couldn't even put her shoes on.

A tall, blonde woman was descending the steps from the minibus. She smiled and waved at Nick. Demelza followed him as he moved nearer the front of the throng.

'Lydia, this is Demelza, the sister in charge of the clinic here.'

Demelza met Lydia's cool gaze. Without her shoes she was smaller than this tall, elegant blonde. How could anybody get off a plane and still look so impeccably groomed? And the flawlessly painted long nails at the end of the outstretched hand were positively intimidating.

Lydia gave a tight little smile, revealing small white teeth, evenly spaced and looking as if they owed some of their symmetry to expensive cosmetic dentistry.

'So you work here? What was your name again?'

'Demelza.'

'What a quaint little name! Foreign, is it? Where do you come from?'

Demelza swallowed, trying to stem the surge of dislike that enveloped her as she stood next to this patronising woman.

'I was born in Cornwall.'

'Ah, the south west of England. I've never been there. Much too far from London for me. I can't stand muddy fields. And I don't suppose you've any decent shops, have you?' she said, casting her eyes disparagingly over Demelza's crumpled sarong.

Demelza stepped back, not deigning to reply to Lydia's ignorant observations. It was a relief that the odious woman was now giving her full attention to her ex-husband.

Lydia was smiling up at Nick. 'I thought you would have brought Ianni to meet me at the airport.'

'He's at school. Actually, he'll be home very shortly and I'd like to get back home for when he arrives.'

Lydia maintained her dazzling smile, spreading her lips even wider at the corners of her brightly painted mouth.

'Oh, well, then, I'll come with you. I'm dying to see my darling little boy! Has he grown since I last saw him?'

Of course he's grown! Demelza thought as she watched Nick's ex-wife simpering up to him. Nick might profess to have no feelings for his wife, but Lydia was certainly making it obvious she still fancied him. Was this visit meant to be an attempt at a reconciliation? The thought drove her spirits down into her bare feet.

'Don't you want to unpack, Lydia?' Nick asked quickly.

'I'd rather see you and Ianni. I haven't come all this way to be on my own. Will you ask that little man over there if he'll put my luggage in my room?'

Demelza was becoming more and more impatient as she watched Nick playing the dutiful husband. Surely he didn't have to be so helpful towards his ex-wife! Not when he'd told her how he couldn't stand the woman. Or had he been exaggerating when he'd described his disastrous marriage? Was the marriage completely over or…?

She deliberately tried to banish that line of thought as she looked across at Nick. He was instructing the tour guide how to handle Lydia's copious, expensive-looking luggage. The tour guide was looking highly put out by the request. Nick put his hand in his pocket and handed over some notes, which seemed to pacify the irate man.

Demelza turned away. She couldn't bear to watch Nick helping out his demanding wife any longer.

'Where's your car, Nick?' Lydia called.

'It's over there under that tree,' Nick said, as he rejoined them.

Lydia gave a tinkling little laugh. 'I'll never climb up to that passenger seat in this narrow skirt, Nick. Give me a hand, will you?'

Nick obligingly hoisted Lydia into the front seat. She was still giggling girlishly as she searched for the seat belt.

'Nick, be a darling and help me with this belt. I never can get the hang of these wretched things.'

Fuming, Demelza climbed into the back, trying to ignore the fact that Nick was now leaning across to fasten Lydia's seat belt. She couldn't bear to see the two of them in such close proximity. She was beginning to wonder if she should be here at all to witness this reunion!

Nick handed Demelza's bag over the seat, without saying a word to her. She began to put on her shoes and pull on her white cotton dress.

'Oh, how quaint!' Lydia said, turning round. 'Do you have to wear that sweet little old-fashioned uniform all the time?'

'Only when I'm on duty,' Demelza said, with steely calm. 'But I didn't bother to change before I went down to the beach. I was feeling tired and simply wanted to relax as soon as possible.'

'We'd just had an emergency,' Nick said, his eyes studiously on the winding road ahead. 'Demelza prevented a tragedy by quickly diagnosing that a small girl was suffering an anaphylactic reaction and giving her the correct treatment.'

'What exciting lives you medical people live! I sometimes wish I'd gone into the medical profession. There was a medical drama I was watching on the television the other evening and—'

'Experiencing medical drama in real life is very different to fiction,' Nick said shortly. 'I think you should stick to modelling, Lydia. How's it going?'

'Fantastic! I'm just about to sign another contract with that London fashion house I told you about. Yes, it's going exceptionally well. It was difficult for me to get away from London, actually, but I thought I simply had to come out and see the men in my life.'

Nick made no comment. He sprang out of the car as soon as he'd parked at the edge of the village, and flung open both doors for his passengers. Demelza jumped down but Lydia appeared to be having great problems with her skirt.

She giggled helplessly. 'Darling, I think you'll have to lift me down! Either that or I'll have to take my skirt off. Take your pick!'

'I think you should keep your clothes on around here, Lydia,' Nick said shortly. 'I'd better lift you down.'

Demelza turned away as Nick raised his arms up towards Lydia.

Lydia's high heels resounded on the ancient cobblestones as the three of them walked along the street towards the villa. Nick paused outside Katerina's house.

'Perhaps you should wait outside for a moment, Lydia. I forgot to tell Ianni that you were coming today and—'

Lydia stared at him. 'You forgot! But I told you ages ago that—'

'I know, but I've been busy and—'

'Daddy!'

Ianni came bounding out through the open door at the sound of Nick's voice. He flung himself against Nick before suddenly pulling away, aware that there was someone else there.

'Hello, Mum,' he said quietly. 'When did you get here?'

'Oh, my little darling! Give Mummy a kiss.' Lydia bent her head downwards but didn't crouch as Nick and Demelza were doing.

Her precious skirt would split if she tried to crouch, Demelza thought as she watched the unlikely reunion between mother and son. Ianni's little body was stiff as he accepted Lydia's kiss on his cheek. Whatever kind of relationship he had with his mother, it certainly wasn't very warm. But it was the relationship between Nick and Lydia that she was worrying about. That was far warmer than she'd been led to believe!

'Well, come on! Show me this family villa I've heard so much about,' Lydia said breezily.

She insisted on being given a guided tour of the whole house, showing special interest in Demelza's top-floor apartment.

'Oh, this is all very cosy, isn't it?' Lydia said, glancing from Nick to Demelza.

'Demelza's a super cook!' Ianni said. 'You should see the fantastic suppers she makes.'

'Well, lucky you!' Lydia said, looking up at her ex-husband. 'A cook and a babysitter on the premises. How long have you been here, Demelza?'

'A couple of months. My contract runs until the end of October.'

'And then you'll go home?'

Demelza was beginning to tire of all this questioning. She knew where it was all leading. The jealous streak in Lydia's nature was patently obvious.

'I may do,' Demelza said evenly. She couldn't help but enjoy the annoyed expression that flitted across Lydia's face. Keep the wretched woman guessing!

She saw that Nick was watching her. He cleared his throat. 'Well, now that you've met Ianni again and seen where we all live, I'll give you a lift back to the resort, Lydia. I expect you'll be wanting to settle in and—'

'I've got a serviced apartment with two bedrooms so that Ianni can come and stay with me,' Lydia announced. 'It's Saturday tomorrow so we can spend all day on the beach, Ianni. How would you like that?'

Ianni glanced up at his father. 'Will you come as well, Dad?'

Nick shook his head. 'No, I can't come. I'll have to go into hospital in the morning. It'll be just you and Mummy,' he finished off, his voice sounding apprehensive. 'You'll like that, won't you?'

Ianni was biting his lip, his eyes downcast. 'Will you come down when you've finished work tomorrow, Dad?'

'I'll come in the evening for a couple of hours when it's cooling down. We can play football or cricket on the beach. Whichever you like. I'll bring everything down with me.'

'And will you come as well, Demelza?' Ianni asked, his eyes beseeching her.

Demelza saw that Lydia was frowning and pursing her lips. She hesitated before answering as she looked up at Nick for some guidance as to what she should do.

'Of course Demelza will come, if she's free,' Nick said quickly. 'I'll take you down, Demelza.'

'OK,' Ianni said, his face brightening.

'Put some of Ianni's things in a bag, Nick,' Lydia said in a cool voice. 'Has he got pyjamas, swimming things, a sweater in case it gets cooler in the evening and—?'

'Goodbye, Lydia,' Demelza said with relief as she went back into her apartment.

She was thinking about poor Ianni as she made herself a cup of tea. It was all too obvious he didn't want to leave Nick. She hoped her favourite little boy wouldn't find the weekend too much of an ordeal. But Lydia was his mother when all was said and done. He should spend time with her. Maybe when mother and son were alone together their relationship would improve.

From what she'd seen, she doubted it, and her heart went out to the boy. He didn't deserve to have a mother like that.

The sun was sinking low in the sky when she heard Nick returning from the resort. Her heart missed a beat as she heard his footsteps on the stone stairs leading up to her terrace. She went to the door to meet him. He looked tired and sad.

'I hated leaving Ianni,' he said quietly.

She held out her arms towards him and he moved into the circle of her embrace, leaning his head down on her shoulder.

'I love that boy so much. I miss him so much when

he's away,' he said slowly. 'But he ought to get to know his mother again. Family is so important.'

She looked up into his eyes and saw the moist, give-away signs that he was hurting inside. Gently, she cupped his chin with her hands and kissed him on the mouth.

For a brief moment he stared at her in surprise and then his strong arms encircled her and he held her tightly against him.

'Demelza, Demelza,' he whispered huskily. 'Some-times I think you really want me as much as I want you, but I'm so afraid I'll frighten you away if I come on too strong.'

She snuggled against his hard chest. The desire surg-ing through her was giving her courage. She had to take the plunge now that she'd given Nick an indica-tion of how she really felt.

'Nick, I've wanted you for so long. I—'

She broke off and looked up at him to judge his reaction. She was surprised to find how easy it was to take the lead now that she'd decided to be completely honest with Nick.

'I want to make love with you, more than anything,' she whispered.

Nick groaned. 'If only I'd known. Why didn't you tell me before? I didn't dare…'

'I didn't know how to…and, anyway, there was never an opportunity. We were never alone long enough…'

'We're alone now,' Nick said, his voice husky with desire. 'And I want you so much, Demelza…'

His hands moved to caress her, slowly, tantalisingly, until she felt she could hold off no longer.

'Let's go inside,' he whispered, as he picked her up in his arms and carried her through to the bedroom.

He laid her on the bed and lay down beside her as he removed her clothes, kissing each new stretch of bare skin as it was revealed. She reached across to him and tore at his clothes, her fingers feeling as if they were all thumbs.

She pressed herself against him, his muscular body tantalising her senses, driving her wild with anticipation. His fingers and lips caressed her until she felt she couldn't contain her longing any longer. And when he entered her, she moved in rhythm with his body, feeling him sink ever deeper inside her until they were fused together in a heavenly sensation of orgasmic love. She cried out as wave after climactic wave swept over her, driving her to heights of ecstasy she hadn't known existed…

The sun was beaming in through the open window when Demelza awoke. Her whole body was tingling in the aftermath of their love. She turned to look at Nick, lying beside her. His dark hair was tousled, and he had one hand above his head in a position she'd seen little Ianni adopt when he'd fallen asleep.

As if sensing her watching him, Nick opened his eyes and gave her a languid smile.

'Come here,' he whispered huskily, as he reached out for her.

She moved into his embrace, revelling in the close feeling of oneness that still lingered from their ecstatic love-making. After their first initial, urgent consummation, they'd made love again…and again…and…

She realised that her recollection of what had happened earlier was very sketchy. It was as if she'd been transported to some heavenly place where the world had ceased to exist except for Nick and herself. They'd been cocooned in an ambience of sensual love which neither of them wanted to leave.

Nick's phone was ringing. He groaned as he scrabbled around at the side of the bed until he found it in his trouser pocket. Demelza thought how boyish he looked, with his hair falling over his face, as he tried to adopt an expression of professional concentration.

'Nick Capodistrias... Ianni! How are you?' He was smiling now as he listened to his son.

Demelza watched as the smile faded. 'Yes, but doesn't Mummy want you to stay? Oh, I see, she's still asleep. Well, don't you think you should wait until she wakes up before...? OK, OK, I'll come down now, Ianni, and sort it out. Don't worry, I'll be with you in a few minutes.'

Nick put down the phone and looked across at Demelza.

'Ianni wants to come home,' he said in a flat voice.

Demelza pulled the sheet up. 'I gathered that. Isn't he happy down there with Lydia?'

'I don't think so. I can't quite make out what the problem is but I'd better go down and sort it out.'

'I'll wait up here until you come back,' Demelza said quietly. 'When you have to go to the hospital Ianni can stay with me. He can have Lefteris round here to play if he'd like to and later we can all go to the beach.'

Nick pulled her back into his arms. 'Thank you for... for being you,' he whispered.

His kiss was gentle but as his lips closed over hers she felt desire stirring again. Quickly, she disentangled herself.

'You'd better go and get Ianni,' she said. 'Otherwise…'

'Don't go away,' he said, swinging his long athletic legs over the side of the bed.

She lay back against the pillows as she listened to him humming to himself in the shower.

He emerged, wrapped in one of her large white towels, looking boyishly handsome and infinitely desirable. She propped herself up against the pillows as she watched him trying to sort out the mound of clothes on the floor.

'Glad your errant landlord fixed the shower,' he told her with a grin. 'What did you have to do to persuade him?'

She laughed. 'Oh, it was easy really. A few bribes and he was putty in my hands.'

'The way I feel this morning, I'd like to build you a huge bathroom, with a Jacuzzi large enough for two and…'

He flung himself back onto the bed but she pushed him away playfully. 'I'm going to start the coffee, so go and get that boy.'

She went out onto the terrace to watch him going down the stairs. He turned at the courtyard door and waved goodbye. She sat for a few moments on the terrace considering what the future now held for her and Nick. They'd crossed the boundary of no return. They were lovers and they could only go forward. They couldn't go back to their comfortable, easygoing platonic relationship.

She leaned back against her chair and held her face up towards the morning sun. She was so happy that Nick had drawn her out of herself, made her feel alive again. She'd been so afraid of signalling that she wanted to move closer to him but last night he'd made it so easy for her.

So easy, and so ecstatically wonderful! She was totally and hopelessly in love with him now. He'd told her how he'd held off showing his true feelings for her because he hadn't wanted to frighten her away.

If he'd only known! She looked out towards the sparkling sea in the distance. 'Hurry back,' she whispered, realising with a pang that her life could never be the same again without Nick.

CHAPTER EIGHT

DEMELZA was humming happily to herself as she tossed the aubergines into a pan. A little oregano perhaps? She sprinkled on some of the herbs that Ianni and Lefteris had gathered with her on the hillside that morning. Stepping back from the cooker, she leaned against the window, taking in the full beauty of the gathering twilight.

She gave a sigh of contentment as she watched Ianni, out there on the terrace, drawing a picture of the impending sunset, his tongue clamped between his teeth in concentration. Before Nick had left to do his evening rounds at the hospital he'd told his son that they could spend the whole day on the beach tomorrow. And they'd had such a marvellous time this afternoon on the beach that Ianni was as thrilled as Demelza was at the prospect of another idyllic day.

She thought back over their wonderful day together. Nick had returned from the resort with a very subdued Ianni who'd refused to give them a clue as to why he didn't want to stay with his mother. All he would say was that he wanted to be with his dad up in the village. After Nick had gone to the hospital, Demelza had told Ianni to go round to Katerina's to call for Lefteris so that she could take both boys up on the hillside to gather herbs.

They'd had such fun up there, calling to the goats with their tinkling bells, patting the donkeys who'd trekked over from the other side of the hill, carrying their heavy loads down to Kopelos town, and eating their midmorning picnic of biscuits still warm from the bakery. And when Nick had come up the path, telling them he'd got back early from the hospital so they could all go to the beach, she'd felt that her happiness was complete.

'I'm going to get some more coloured pencils from downstairs, Demelza,' Ianni called. 'There's a special red colour that would be brilliant for the sun, if I can find it. OK?'

'Fine! But don't be too long. Daddy will be back soon.'

She clasped a hand over her heart which seemed to be swelling with joy. This was the exact scenario she'd always dreamed of. A calm domestic situation shared with a wonderful, loving man, an adorable child who—

Her blissful thoughts vanished as a figure appeared at the top of the stairs. There was no mistaking that long, expensively styled blonde hair. Her spirits sank.

She moved quickly out through the open door.

'Hello, Lydia. You've just missed Ianni. He's gone downstairs for something. And Nick's at the hospital. He should be back soon so—'

'It's you I wanted to see,' Lydia said in a steely voice, as she sank down onto one of the chairs on the terrace. 'I was hoping to find you alone. If Nick's due back soon, I'll come straight to the point.'

Demelza moved towards the table and sat down on the opposite side from her unwanted visitor.

Lydia's eyes flickered ominously as she looked across the table. 'This is a very cosy little set-up, isn't it? How convenient for you to move in with the boss.'

Demelza bridled. 'I'll ignore that remark, but don't

waste any more of my time, Lydia. Why have you come here?'

Lydia bared her dazzling white teeth in an approximation of a sugary smile. 'I'm Ianni's mother, remember? Or had you conveniently forgotten? My only concern is for his welfare. Something that you seem to disregard entirely.'

Demelza gasped. 'How dare you? Ianni is like a son to me and—'

'Exactly!' Lydia's eyes flashed triumphantly. 'That's why I'm here. I know what your game is but it won't work. I came out here for a reconciliation with Nick. Did you know he actually invited me to come here to see if we could get back together again? He phoned me to say that Ianni was missing me and he wanted us to be a family again.'

'I find that very hard to believe,' Demelza said evenly. 'Nick has always led me to believe that it was over between you.'

Lydia gave a harsh laugh. 'Well, he would say that, wouldn't he? Nick's one of the boys. Always happy to have a bit on the side. He's a full-blooded man, for God's sake! How else could he manage without a wife if he didn't find himself a girlfriend to satisfy his insatiable lust? Oh, and he's got plenty of that, hasn't he? Don't you find he's fantastic in bed, Demelza?'

Demelza stood up, her eyes blazing with anger. 'I think you should go now, Lydia.'

Lydia remained rooted to her chair. 'Not until I've said what I came to say. When I was married to Nick I took exception to him having other girlfriends. That's why I chose to divorce him. But now I've come to realise that was a mistake. Some men...lusty, super-sexy men like Nick...need more than one woman to satisfy them. So when we get married again, as we will, I'll be prepared to overlook his philandering. But until we're back together as a family, I'm not going to tolerate any opposition.'

Demelza leaned both hands on the table and glared at Lydia. 'That wasn't what Nick told me. According to him, you were the one who was always having affairs.'

'Hah! Well, Nick would say that, wouldn't he? He's not going to admit that he was the one who always loved his little bit of extra excitement. But family is family and Nick knows where his duty lies. Very strong on family is Nick…'

Demelza drew in her breath. It was as if a cold breeze had suddenly blown over the terrace. She was trying not to believe what Lydia was telling her but the part about Nick's insistence that the family was all-important struck an unpleasant chord with her. She remembered that was a fact he'd stressed when they'd chatted together.

Lydia's relentlessly strident voice was continuing. 'Nick was reluctant to break up the family before and he's seen what splitting up has done to Ianni. That's why he wants me back. And that's why I want you to clear off and leave us to get our family life together again. Ianni needs a mother, his true birth mother. So stop pushing your nose in where you're not wanted. If you have any feelings for little Ianni, then let him have his real mother back. Nick and I made this family, not you!'

Lydia stood up quickly. Her wrought-iron chair fell backwards with a loud clanging sound. Demelza noticed how the noise echoed eerily around the silent hillside as if sounding the knell of her dreams. Had Nick really asked Lydia to come out to the island for a reconciliation? Was she herself simply just his 'little bit on the side'?

Lydia paused at the top of the stairs and turned round, narrowing her eyes as she glared at Demelza. 'Think about it before you carry on this wicked affair with Ianni's father. How would you like it if somebody was trying to break up your family?'

'But you're divorced!' Demelza flung back at her.

'All a mistake, I assure you. I should have been more tolerant with my straying husband. I've learned my lesson and when we get back together again I won't make the same mistake twice.'

Demelza found she was trembling as she watched Lydia going down the stairs. She held her breath until the courtyard door closed behind her and then she sank down onto the nearest chair and put her hands over her face.

A tiny hand touching her shoulder made her jump. 'Ianni! You're back! Did you find the crayon you wanted?'

Ianni's eyes were solemn as he nodded. 'What did Mummy want? I waited until she'd gone before I came back. I thought she'd come to take me away.'

What a sad thing for a child to say! Demelza brushed a hand over her damp eyes. Was she herself adding to Ianni's misery by confusing him as to where his loyalty should lie?

'Mummy called in to see me about something but she was in a hurry. That's why she didn't wait around to see you and Daddy.'

She heard the courtyard door opening and Nick called out, 'I'm home!'

Oh, what a welcome sound! Demelza leapt to her

feet and ran to the top of the stairs to wait for him. As he reached the top step he held out his arms and folded them around her. She went willingly into his embrace, Ianni clinging tightly to both of them.

But moments later she pulled herself away as she remembered this was exactly the sort of behaviour that was splitting up Ianni's natural family. She couldn't go on playing surrogate mother to Ianni and wife to Nick. If Nick really wanted to resurrect his marriage and she herself was simply the other woman, shouldn't she back off and allow Ianni to get to know his natural mother again?

She walked purposefully towards the open door of her apartment. 'I was cooking supper for all of us, but if you'd rather go out…'

Nick was right behind her, his arms on her shoulders. 'Of course I don't want to go out when you've cooked supper. There's nothing I like better than being here with you, just the three of us, and—'

'Nick!'

She swung herself around and looked up into his dark eyes. How she loved him! It was agony to contemplate ever living without him, but did she have the right to continue her affair with him?

'Nick, don't you think you should take Ianni down to the resort and spend some time with Lydia? After all, she's made the effort to come out here. Maybe if you took Ianni with you he would get used to his mother again. It's bound to be difficult for him when—'

'Hey! What's this all about?' Nick pulled her against him and held her so close she could hear the beating of his heart. 'Ianni wants to stay here and so do I. Unless you're fed up with us. In which case…'

She raised her eyes to his. 'I want you here with me,' she said quietly. 'But maybe you should try to patch things up with Lydia...for Ianni's sake.'

'I think we should stay here,' Nick said firmly as he sat down at the table next to his son. 'Wow! That's a beautiful picture you've done, Ianni!'

Ianni smiled. 'It's for Demelza.'

Demelza sank down at the other side of the little boy and put her hand on his shoulder. 'Thank you very much. I'll put it on the wall in my living room where everyone can see it.'

'Now, how about doing a picture for Mummy to take with you when you go down to see her on Monday?' Nick said.

'Do I have to go?' Ianni asked plaintively. 'I want to stay up here with Demelza.'

Nick turned to look at Demelza. Was it her imagination or did he look uneasy?

'I've agreed to take Ianni down to spend the morning with his mother,' he said in a careful, casual tone. 'Now that the school holidays are here he'll have more time to play and Lydia was upset that he didn't want to stay on with her this morning. So I've agreed to take him down for a few hours each day while she's here. It's important for him to get to know his mother again. Family ties are so important.'

Demelza felt her spirits plummeting. Yes, it was important for Ianni to get to know his mother again, especially if Nick and Lydia were planning a reconciliation.

'But I can come back here to sleep, can't I?' Ianni asked.

'Of course you can,' Nick said.

Demelza stood up. 'I'll go and get supper ready.'

'And afterwards we can go down to Giorgio's, join in the Saturday night fun. What do you say, Demelza?' Nick called after her.

She put on a bright smile. 'Fine!'

As Demelza listened to the haunting Greek music in Giorgio's taverna she found it impossible to recapture the excitement she'd experienced on that first evening here. Now that she'd fallen in love with Nick, the whole scenario had changed. She'd had no idea what kind of a relationship she'd been heading for. And when she'd finally overcome her fear and apprehension it had been only to discover that she was destined to be the other woman, not the main person in Nick's life.

That was, if Lydia was to be believed. Only time would tell. Nick seemed already to be taking steps to include his ex-wife back in his life.

'You haven't drunk your wine. Are you feeling OK?'

Nick's concerned voice interrupted her thoughts. She forced herself to smile up at him.

'I'm fine. A bit tired, but it's been a long day. And it's so hot. It doesn't even get much cooler in the evenings now.'

'But you're still happy out here, aren't you?'

She revelled in the tender expression in his eyes. 'I love it.'

'You don't have to go back when your contract runs out in October. We need another experienced nursing sister in the hospital. Why don't you stay on?'

The thought of remaining here indefinitely with Nick was very tempting, but not if he was planning a reconciliation with Lydia. And not if he needed to have

more than one woman, as his ex-wife had insisted...and she should know!

Her dream was to have Nick all to herself and she
wouldn't compromise. Until now he'd seemed the sort
of man who would be totally committed to the woman
he loved but, then, she'd only known him a few weeks.
Was that long enough to find out his faults? Probably
not. They were still in the honeymoon period. A honeymoon without any hope of a wedding!

She looked at little Ianni who had fallen asleep in
Nick's arms. 'I think we should take Ianni home,' she
said quietly.

'Let him sleep here for a while,' Nick said. 'Anna
has finished her cooking. She loves to care for him.'

Demelza looked across the room to where Nick's
kind, motherly aunt was watching them. As if sensing
what they were saying, she moved between the tables
to join them.

'Go and dance with Demelza, Nick,' she said, in her
fascinatingly accented English, reaching down to take
her great-nephew in her arms. 'Leave Ianni with me.
He looks so like your father when he is asleep.'

She turned to smile at Demelza as she cradled the
little boy against her. 'Nick's father, Andreas, was a
handsome boy, just like little Ianni. He was five years
younger than me and I used to look after him when my
mother was busy in the kitchen. I would take him down
to the harbour to watch the fishing boats coming in
and...'

Anna broke off as her voice choked. 'Yes, I loved
my little brother. And then when he grew up he was
so handsome—all the girls wanted to be his girlfriend.
The village girls didn't like it when he fell in love with
Lucy—that was Nick's English mother. But I was

happy about it, because she was a beautiful girl and she adored my Andreas so I didn't mind that she took him away from me. But when Andreas was drowned in the storm...'

Once more Anna had to pause. She pulled a tissue from the pocket of her voluminous cotton skirt and dabbed her eyes before continuing, 'When Andreas was lost at sea I thought my heart would break. But there was little Nick to remind me of my brother, and later on my little Ianni. Leave me here with him, Demelza. Nick is longing to dance with you.'

Nick leaned across. 'What are you two whispering about?'

'I was telling your lovely Demelza some of our family history,' Anna said. 'Go and dance and let me spend some time with Ianni.'

Nick held out his hand and drew Demelza to her feet before leading her away from the table.

The small three-piece group of musicians had struck up a soulfully slow dance after several loud, lively pieces. Nick pulled Demelza closely against him as they moved across the uneven flagstones that served as a dance floor. She could feel the beating of his heart against hers and the conflict inside her increased. Should she compromise and go with the flow? Should she take what little part of Nick's life he was willing to share?

For the moment the only decision she would make was to make no decision on the future! She hadn't had time to recover from Lydia's shock announcement about the possibility of a reconciliation. Maybe when she'd had more time she would be able to assess the situation without emotion creeping in to cloud her judgement. But until she knew if this reconciliation was really on the cards she must try to pretend it wasn't going to happen.

'You're looking very solemn,' Nick whispered, his lips close to her ear. 'What's the matter?'

She took a deep breath. 'I was thinking about Ianni having to go down to see his mother on Monday. How long is Lydia planning to stay out here?'

She watched in alarm as a veiled expression removed the tenderness from Nick's eyes.

He hesitated. 'I really don't know. She's planning to stay on longer than we initially anticipated.'

'But I thought she had an important modelling contract to go back to.'

'I think she's completely freelance so she can please herself,' he said in an even tone. 'When I was talking to her this morning she said she was going to stay on longer than she'd intended. Anyway, why all this concern about Lydia? I know you don't like her but that's understandable. She has that effect on most women. Something to do with the model image, I suppose. But you won't have to see much of her.'

'Will you?' she asked evenly.

He raised an eyebrow. 'Will I what?'

'Have to see much of her?'

He held her at arm's length in front of him. 'That's a funny question. I'll have to see her when I take Ianni down, of course. She's really making an effort to get to know him again, and after all she's his natural mother. So, genetically, they must have something in common. It would be nice if they could get together again.'

She swallowed hard. 'Yes, it would.'

'Now, come on, stop worrying about Lydia. Relax!'

He pulled her against him once more and she weakened as the feel of his muscular body against hers sent shivers down her spine. She remembered how they'd made love together in that out-of-this-world experience which had lasted all night. How could she possibly deny herself the joys of their love-making now that she knew what it was like to lie in Nick's arms? She couldn't call a halt to this affair just because there was the possibility of a reconciliation between Lydia and Nick.

She had to fight to keep Nick! But only if it wasn't going to harm Ianni. If Ianni's place was with his real mother in his natural family unit then that changed everything.

One day at a time! She couldn't bear to look too far into the future.

They walked slowly back along the deserted village street, Ianni cradled in Nick's arms, sleeping peacefully. As they reached the courtyard, Nick stopped and looked down at Demelza.

'Will you sleep with me in my apartment tonight, Demelza?' he asked, his voice tender and husky with emotion.

She looked down at the sleeping child and shook her head. 'I wouldn't want Ianni to wake up and find me in your bed.'

'But Ianni accepts you as if you were his mother and—'

'Shh! I'm not Ianni's mother and I don't want to confuse him. He's a little boy who already has a mother, a mother who's trying to get to know him again.'

It was breaking her heart to say these things but she felt that she had to take a stance. It would be so easy now to snuggle up beside Nick, to feel his arms around her, to lie there in the morning, satiated with their love-making, pretending that she was the only person in Nick's life who counted for anything, other than Ianni. She could pretend she was Ianni's mother but deep down she would feel a terrible guilt for trying to steal Lydia's child away from her.

'Goodnight, Nick,' she said quietly.

She noticed the sadness in his eyes as he stooped to kiss her lightly on the lips. The confusion of her emotions continued as she hurried up the stairs and made her way into her own apartment. She expected to feel at peace with herself for having made the decision to back off.

But she didn't.

As the long, hot summer days continued with cloudless skies and relentless sun, Demelza found that she was having to deal with far too many cases of sunburn. In spite of her talks and discussions with the incoming tourists about the danger of over-exposure to the sun's damaging rays, there were still people who came out for a week, expecting to go back to the UK with a golden tan. She'd had to hospitalise two patients already and one of them had been so badly burned that he'd had to postpone his flight home.

It was now midway through August so there were many weeks to go before the cooler days of October would be upon them. She leaned forward to sort out the case notes on her desk. It had been a busy morning but everything was quiet now. This afternoon she would be able to relax and that was when she would start to worry again about her relationship with Nick.

Since Lydia had asked her to keep out of Nick's and

Ianni's life her emotions had been in turmoil. On the one hand her instinct was to fight, but on the other her love for little Ianni made her more cautious. If Nick really was planning to get his natural family back together again then it would be utterly wrong of her to interfere.

Nick was still as attentive and loving towards her, but she'd made a point of holding off making love with him since Lydia's revelations. She'd hoped that the situation would have been resolved one way or another by now, but she still felt that she was in a state of limbo.

Glancing out of the window towards the beach, she found herself holding her breath. As if to confuse her even further, she could see Lydia out there, walking down to the sea. Ianni was with her, holding her hand. And in the other hand he was carrying a brand-new football.

Nick had given Demelza a lift down to the beach resort this morning when he'd brought Ianni to be with his mother. She remembered how Lydia had rushed to the car park when they'd arrived, her make-up flawless, wearing a fabulous designer-looking sundress and the inevitable high-heeled strappy sandals. She'd reached up to put her arms around Nick's neck and kiss him on the cheek. And then she'd given Ianni the new football, which had made him whoop with delight.

Demelza could still hear his cries of happiness as he'd demanded to go straight to the beach.

'Come to the restaurant with me first, darling, for some breakfast,' Lydia had cooed. 'You can have ice cream if you like and...'

Demelza shivered at the disturbing recollections. Since Lydia's arrival last month, she had showered her

son with presents and Ianni seemed less reluctant now
to spend some of his days with her. His days, but never
his nights. For some reason known only to Ianni, he
refused to stay down at the expensive apartment Lydia
was renting now for an indeterminate period. Nick had
continued to bring Ianni down to the apartment several
times a week and Demelza couldn't help but wonder
how he was getting on with his ex-wife now that he
was seeing so much of her.

She tried to tell herself that sooner or later she would
find out just how real or false this reconciliation was
going to be, but it didn't help her to contain her impatience. A couple of times she'd felt like challenging
Nick, asking him to come clean about his intentions
towards Lydia, but at the last minute she'd managed to
restrain herself from upsetting the rapport that existed
between them. She had no right to expect him to be
faithful to her and therefore she should allow their relationship to drift along with no demands on either
side.

It was always wonderful to be with Nick, even
though she spent half the time torturing herself with
thoughts that it couldn't last. For the moment she had
to be content with whatever time they could spend together.

The ringing of the phone interrupted her thoughts.
'Sister Demelza here...Yes, Nick...'

She leaned back against her chair to enjoy listening
to the sound of his voice. 'Yes, I've just finished,' she
told him. 'I can come over to the hospital if you need
me.'

It was wonderful to be needed by Nick! She could
feel her toes tingling in that special way that happened
whenever she was going to meet him. The fact that this

was a purely professional situation didn't make any difference.

Nick was waiting for her in his office as arranged. He'd been deliberately professional over the phone and she'd gathered that he'd had a patient with him at the time. He stood up when she went in and motioned towards one of the seats at the other side of his desk.

'You know Bryony Driver, don't you?' he said, referring to the patient who was sitting in the other chair.

Demelza smiled as she recognised the woman who'd come to her clinic back in May, suffering from depression.

'How are you, Bryony? You're looking much better than when I last saw you.'

Bryony smiled back. 'I feel great! That psychiatrist you put me on to has worked wonders.'

'Glad to hear it. It was Dr Capodistrias who found him for us. Are you still having treatment?'

Nick leaned forward across his desk. 'That's what we're here to discuss. Bryony is insisting that she doesn't want any more sessions with Dr Michaelis, but I'm suggesting to her that it's too soon to consider herself fully cured. And as Bryony is also your patient, Sister, I felt I should consult you. The problem is that Bryony hasn't even finished the first course of treatment and—'

'Excuse me, Dr Capodistrias,' Bryony interrupted. 'Now that Sister Demelza is here I can tell you the real reason. I wanted you both to know what was happening.'

Their patient hesitated as she looked first at Nick and then at Demelza, as if to judge their reactions.

'You see, I've met a man...a wonderful man...

We're having an affair and I don't want him to find out I'm seeing a psychiatrist. I don't want him to think there's something wrong with me. Dr Michaelis wants me to continue treatment, but I don't think it's necessary any more. I feel so happy!'

'I'm glad you feel happy again, Bryony,' Demelza said gently. 'Are you still taking your tranquillisers?'

Bryony gave her a dazzling smile. 'No, that's the best part about it. I stopped taking them in June, two weeks after I met Costas, and I haven't had any since. I'm ecstatic! It's the best thing that ever happened to me.'

Nick stood up and came round to their side of the desk. He stood looking down at Bryony, his expression guarded.

'Are you talking about Costas who owns the fish restaurant, down in the harbour?'

Bryony nodded happily. 'Do you know him?'

'I've known him since we were children. We're about the same age. His wife died a couple of years ago and his mother has been helping him to look after the two children.'

'They're lovely little boys,' Bryony said, her voice warm with enthusiasm. 'I've always wanted kids of my own but my husband wasn't keen on the idea. Anyway, they've really taken to me and I think it won't be long before Costas asks me to marry him. The point is, I don't want anyone to tell him I've been seeing Dr Michaelis about my depression. I'm not depressed any more and I just want to get on with my new life.'

'I understand how you feel, Bryony, and I'm very happy for you,' Demelza said carefully. 'But are you sure that Costas feels as happy as you do about this relationship?'

'Of course he does! You should see us together!
We're both very much in love. That's why I want to
finish my treatment with Dr Michaelis and I don't want
anybody to know I've been one of his patients.'

'I'll have a discreet chat with him,' Nick said, 'and
we'll take you off his list of patients. But if ever you
feel you need to see him again…'

Bryony gave him a beaming smile. 'That's wonderful. Don't worry, I won't need to see Dr Michaelis
again. And you won't breathe a word to anyone, will
you, Doctor?'

'Absolutely not!' Nick said solemnly.

'Thank you both for all your help.' Bryony stood up,
shook hands with them and hurried out of the door, her
feet in their high-heeled sandals barely touching the
ground.

Demelza turned to look at Nick. He leaned forward
and took hold of both her hands.

'The power of love!' he said, his voice husky with
emotion.

'Magic, isn't it?' Demelza breathed. 'But do you
think it will last?'

Nick shrugged. 'Who can say? Who can ever predict
the future?'

Demelza felt this was all too close to home. 'This
Costas, is he an honourable sort of man? I mean, he's
not just stringing Bryony along, is he? She's a very
vulnerable, unstable woman, and I wouldn't like to see
her hurt again. She had a rotten experience because of
her husband's infidelity and another disappointment
could push her over the edge.'

Nick's eyes flickered. 'Costas is as honourable as
any man I know. But, having said that, who am I to
judge someone's character? He's never done anything

dishonourable before. As far as I know, he was always faithful to his wife. But that doesn't mean he might be unfaithful in the future if he and Bryony get married. You've got to take a chance with love. There are no certainties in life, are there?'

Demelza suppressed a shiver. Was Nick trying to tell her something? She lived in fear of the day that he might tell her he was going to take Lydia back as his wife.

'Bryony will have to take one day at a time and enjoy her present happiness while it lasts,' Demelza said quietly.

'Hey, don't sound so pessimistic!' Nick said. 'It could last for ever.'

She put on the bright smile that always helped to cover up her true feelings. 'It could indeed.'

He leaned forward and pulled her gently to her feet so that he could cradle her in his arms. She felt herself relaxing against him, revelling in the feel of his strong athletic body so close to hers. If only she could be sure, if only...

'I needed to see you about something else, Demelza,' he whispered. 'I don't know what's been troubling you lately but it seems ages since we were alone together, really alone.'

'Nick, I—'

'No, listen for a moment. You've always got some excuse to make when I want you to spend some time with me. Your main concern seems to be that Ianni shouldn't find us together in a...well, an intimate situation. But tonight he's going to stay with Anna and Giorgio. They're putting on a birthday party for one of their grandchildren and they're having the Greek equivalent of a sleepover. I'd like to take you out to that new restaurant that's just opened by the harbour and then, maybe afterwards…just maybe…no promises… you would come home with me and we could be alone…really alone…'

Nick was looking down at her with that plaintive expression that little Ianni used when he was bent on getting his own way. Demelza reached up and pushed the wayward lock of hair away from his forehead so that she could fully appreciate the tender expression in his dark, searching eyes.

'I'd love to,' she whispered, deliberately ignoring the small voice of warning that constantly nagged her when she allowed herself to follow her heart's desires.

Slowly, he bent his head and kissed her on the lips, gently at first and then with an all-consuming passion that gave her a hint of what was to come later.

Pulling himself away, his eyes searched her face. 'Don't change your mind before this evening, will you, Demelza?'

She smiled. 'Why should I change my mind?'

He hesitated. 'Well, you seem so unpredictable at the moment. I don't understand you.'

'I don't understand you either,' she countered.

'We'll have to do something about that,' he said gently. 'But not here. Tonight…'

CHAPTER NINE

FROM where Demelza was sitting at their window-seat table, looking across the room and out through the open kitchen door of the harbourside taverna, she could see the succulent roast lamb cooking on the slowly turning spit. The fragrant aroma of the meat and herbs was making her feel very hungry as she waited for their meal to be served.

'Have some more olives,' Nick said, passing the plate across the table. 'You're probably starving, like me.'

Demelza smiled. 'Just realised I missed lunch. I got called out to see a patient in one of the resort rooms when I got back from the hospital. A young woman with asthma. She was gasping for breath when I got there so I gave her some oxygen while I checked on her medication. It turned out she'd just arrived that morning after a night flight and forgotten to take it. I stayed with her for a couple of hours until we got her breathing under control.'

'So you'll be able to eat your fair share of this special lamb they're serving. They like people with good appetites here, so I'm told. I've been looking forward to trying this place out but there was never an opportunity when we were both free.'

'You could have brought Lydia,' she said.

Nick raised an eyebrow. 'I don't know why you keep talking about Lydia. Tonight it's just us, remember?'

Demelza smiled. 'I hadn't forgotten.'

If only she could forget Lydia altogether! If only the wretched woman had stayed out of their lives, remained quietly divorced, out of sight and across the sea somewhere, keeping her flawlessly painted, immaculately manicured, useless hands off the man she herself loved!

She took a deep breath. Nick had said that tonight was for the two of them and she was going to go along with that. She was going to concentrate solely on this wonderful man, who was watching her with that quizzical gaze that told her he didn't know what to expect next from her.

'It's a great taverna,' she said, looking around her. 'I love the view of the harbour, with all the twinkling lights on the boats. We're so near the water I could almost reach out and dip my hand in it.'

Nick grinned. 'Why don't you? I'll hold your legs while you lean through the window.'

She laughed spontaneously at the mischievous expression on Nick's face. It was so good to be with him again and have him entirely to herself. He made her laugh, though sometimes he made her feel like crying because she loved him so much and she had to remind herself that until she knew what was really going on between Lydia and him, he was unobtainable.

She looked out across the calm water of the harbour at the little boats bobbing on the surface of the moonlit water. All around the harbour different strains of music floated out to blend with the happy voices of the evening revellers. Kopelos was such a magic place! The sort of place she'd like to live for the rest of her life...if only that were possible...

'You've got that look again,' he teased. 'Happy yet sad at the same time. What's worrying you now?'

'Nothing!' she said lightly. 'I'm only worried that I might die of starvation before the food arrives… Ah, here it is!'

They clinked their wineglasses together before beginning on the succulent lamb.

'Mmm, that's delicious!' Demelza said, as the delicate, tasty morsel seemed to melt in her mouth. 'And the beans are cooked just as I like them, slightly al dente so that they haven't lost any of their flavour.'

Nick reached across and topped up her wineglass.

'Hey, careful. I don't want you to have to carry me out to the car.'

Nick gave her a rakish grin. 'It's not very far and you don't weigh much, so don't worry.'

A couple of waiters were now dancing at one end of the taverna, explaining their intricate steps to the admiration of the tourists who were being encouraged to join in. The lively music was adding to Demelza's feeling of euphoria. She looked across the table and saw that Nick was watching her. He reached across and took hold of her hand.

'Are you happy now?'

She smiled as she nodded. 'It's good to get away…by ourselves.'

'I think so,' he said, his voice suddenly solemn.

'Nick…'

She hesitated as she realised that this wasn't the moment to spoil everything by asking him outright what his intentions were towards Lydia. What would she achieve if he were to tell her that for the sake of the natural family he was going to have another shot at marriage with Lydia? What she didn't know wouldn't harm her for this evening. And if he were to say the idea was preposterous he would still be annoyed at her for raising the subject.

'Yes?'

He was waiting for her to say something. Quickly she improvised. 'I'm glad that Ianni has family he can be with on the island. As an only child he could have been lonely, but he's got aunts, great aunts, cousins…'

She watched the expression in Nick's eyes change. 'One of my greatest wishes is that he won't be an only child. Some time in the future I hope he'll have brothers and sisters.'

She swallowed hard. Was that a strong enough reason for Nick to attempt a reconciliation with his ex-wife?

A waiter was placing a plate of oranges in the middle of their table. 'On the house!' he said, smiling down at them. 'And would you like some coffee?'

Nick ordered small cups of Greek coffee which Demelza had come to enjoy over the months she'd been on the island.

'When I first arrived, this coffee used to taste bitter to me, but now I love it,' she said, as she sipped the thick, dark liquid.

'We'll make an islander of you yet,' Nick said. 'Have you thought any more about taking a sister's post at the hospital when your contract runs out at the end of October?'

'When do I have to tell you?' she asked quickly.

'I'll need to know by mid-September, otherwise we'll have to advertise the post. There's no one here on the island who could fill it.'

'I'll let you know as soon as I've decided.'

'What is there to decide? I thought you loved the life out here?'

'I do!' She drew in her breath. 'But I have to be sure it…it would be right for me. Give me time.'

And give me some indication of what your intentions are! She looked across the table and felt her heart turning over with love for this unpredictable man. What exactly was he planning for the women in his life? As soon as she knew that, she could act, but until her position in his life became clearer she wasn't going to commit herself. There was no way she was going to stay on as the other woman!

She remained quiet as Nick drove up the hill to the village after their meal. He parked the car at the end of the village street, taking hold of her hand as they strolled along towards the villa. Once inside the courtyard he turned towards her and took her in his arms.

'You haven't changed your mind about staying with me, have you?' he whispered huskily.

She looked up into his eyes, liquid with tenderness. 'No, I haven't changed my mind,' she said softly, as the wonderful shivers of anticipation began to run down her spine.

Tonight was for the two of them. She would pretend that no one else existed in their lives.

He scooped her up into his arms as he carried her over the threshold of his apartment, setting her down only when they'd reached the bedroom. She reached for him as he made to leave her, pulling him down beside her as all her pent-up passion and frustration began to drive her wild with desire. His eyes registered surprise and then delight at her obvious longing for him.

He ran his hands lightly over her, removing her dress, gently at first and then with a great urgency that matched her own impatience to feel their naked skin pressed against each other. She tore at the buttons on his shirt, so that her breasts could feel the muscles of his chest and his pounding heart. Their clothes were scattered on the bed and the floor in their desperate demand for fulfilment.

With her naked body pressed against him, Demelza could feel the urgency of Nick's love for her. Every fibre of her being was in tune with his as he thrust himself inside her and drove her to a wild delirium of rhythmic ecstasy as he moved in that primaeval, tantalising way that turned her body into liquid fire.

And as she climaxed, she cried out with savage abandon as she assumed a completely new self, a new being without any worldly cares, living only for the present on another heavenly planet.

Later they slept, only to awaken again so that they could once more consummate their love. And as the first light of dawn crept over the window-sill, Demelza curled up against Nick, knowing without a shadow of a doubt that this was where she wanted to be for the rest of her life.

The sun was already warm on her skin when Demelza finally regained full consciousness and decided she ought to try to get back into the real world. But even as she stretched her arms above her head in an attempt to gain some kind of normality, Nick pulled her against him and began caressing her body with renewed urgency.

'Nick, I have to think about getting out of bed,' she whispered as his sensual fingers began to undermine her resolve.

'So have I,' he said, softly as he kissed her skin. 'But later...much later...'

*   *   *

It was the ringing of the phone that woke her. Demelza glanced at the clock as Nick answered it and was shocked to see how late it was. She grabbed her mobile and phoned Irini at the clinic. Irini wasn't in the least bit worried when Demelza explained that she would be late that morning. There was nothing that she couldn't handle by herself, the competent nurse told Demelza. She was to take her time about getting down to the clinic if she had problems.

Demelza finished her conversation just as Nick was saying goodbye to the sister who'd phoned him from the hospital.

'One of my post-operative patients is haemorrhaging,' Nick said briskly, as he leapt out of bed and began extricating his clothes from the pile on the floor. 'I've got to get over there as soon as I can. Do you think you could could collect Ianni from Anna's and take him down to the beach resort with you? Lydia's expecting him again this morning so—'

'Of course!'

She was firmly back in the everyday world. Duty was calling in every direction. There was only the tantalising tingling of her skin to remind her that she'd spent the night in an idyllic paradise with the most wonderful man in the world.

She hauled herself out of bed and grabbed the nearest garment, which happened to be Nick's towelling robe.

He bent over her as she knotted the belt. 'Very fetching! If you weren't knotting that so tightly I might...'

She gave him a whimsical smile as she looked up into his eyes. 'You'd better get a move on. Don't worry about Ianni. I'll look after him at the clinic if Lydia has other things to do this morning.'

'Thanks.' He kissed her lightly on the mouth and hurried to the door.

She listened to his footsteps in the courtyard until the clanging of the outside gate told her that he was gone. For a few moments she sat on the edge of the bed, allowing herself the simple luxury of a day-dream…a daydream where she was married to Nick, where she spent every night snuggled up next to him, making love whenever they felt like it. And in the dream there were more children besides Ianni…at least two more… A baby girl perhaps…

She gave herself a firm shake and hurried away into the shower. As the warm water cascaded over her, she felt herself returning to normality. She couldn't live in this fantasy world any longer, much as she would like to remain there for ever. Her problems wouldn't be resolved by dreaming…

Anna was delighted to see Demelza when she turned up on the doorstep of the house adjoining Giorgio's taverna.

'*Kali mera*, Demelza! Good morning.'

Demelza smiled. '*Kali mera*, Anna.'

Anna took hold of Demelza's arm. 'Come in. I've just made some coffee…yes, you've got time for cof-fee. Always in so much hurry, not good for you. This is Kopelos, not England. Ianni is still in his pyjamas upstairs. Sit down. I baked some little cakes today. Try one—this one with some of my home-made apricot jam…'

It was impossible to hurry away from Anna's house.

Demelza decided to take Irini at her word and take her time in getting down to the resort.

'No problem about your clinic,' Anna assured her. 'Giorgio will run you down to the beach resort when you finish your coffee.'

Demelza could feel Anna's eyes on her as she sipped her coffee. The older woman leaned forward in conspiratorial fashion, lowering her voice to say, 'How do you like Lydia, that ex-wife of Nick's?'

'Er…' Demelza looked across at Anna as she sought the right words. But there was no need for words as her hesitation spoke volumes.

'Exactly!' Anna said, in a triumphant tone. 'You don't have to tell me what you think about that woman because I can see it in your eyes. Why Nick ever married her I shall never know. It was a mistake right from the start. We all knew it wouldn't last. I was so happy when I heard they'd split up…not happy for little Ianni, of course, but Nick is a good father.'

Demelza swallowed the piece of cake in her mouth and took another sip of coffee. She liked this aunt of Nick's. They were united in their dislike of Lydia and their love of Nick. It would do no harm to open up her heart to this older, probably wiser woman.

'Yes, Nick is certainly a good father,' Demelza said carefully. 'But do you think it's enough for a child to have only one parent? Lydia told me that Nick had asked her for a reconciliation so that they could be a family again.'

'Never!' Anna said, banging her hand down on the table so that the cups and saucers rattled.

'My Nico would never want to be with that treacherous woman again. She's lying to you if she says Nick wants her back. She must be up to her old tricks again.

All she wanted when she married Nick was a...how do you say it in English? A meal ticket. A man to pay the bills so that she didn't need to earn any money herself.'

'I thought Lydia had a successful career as a model,' Demelza said innocently, still fishing for more information.

'Career? What career? She won a beauty competition in a small town when she was eighteen. Since then she's had one or two jobs in department stores, modelling the new clothes for a day or two, but nothing that paid any real money. She invents stories about modelling contracts but it's all lies. The only job she's ever had is shopping for the clothes that will make her look good and painting her face to try and make herself look younger.'

Demelza leaned back in her chair. 'So you don't think that Nick wants a reconciliation?'

'Absolutely not! But Lydia wants him back so she'll stop at nothing.'

'Thanks, Anna,' Demelza said, quietly. 'You've set my mind at rest. Lydia told me to back off so that I wouldn't upset Ianni's chances of family life, but now...'

'The only family life that Ianni needs is with you and Nick. I'll be honest with you, Demelza. It was my idea to ask Ianni to stay in our house last night because I thought it was time you and Nick had some...how do you say it in English? Quality time, I think. I've watched the two of you together and I know you were made for each other. Just as I knew the same thing when I watched Nick's father, my precious brother Andreas, with his beautiful English Lucy. Now, that really was a marriage made in heaven…which is where they both are now…'

Anna grabbed a tissue and dabbed at her eyes. 'Promise me you'll make my Nico happy by marrying him. I know—'

'Anna, you're jumping to conclusions,' Demelza said gently. 'Nick and I are just good friends at the moment…well, perhaps a little bit more…'

Anna was smiling. 'A lot more! You didn't get that happy-with-the-world glow that you've got this morning from having an early night in your own bed! So when Nico asks you to—'

'I need to know the truth about Nick's relationship with Lydia first.'

'The relationship is dead. Ask Nico. Go on, ask him…'

'It's not as easy as that, Anna. I don't want to force him into— Hi, Ianni!'

It was a relief for Demelza that Ianni had appeared to save her from what was fast becoming an embarrassing situation. Anna was seeing the delicate situation in black and white whereas there were many grey areas that needed sorting out.

Ianni ran into Demelza's arms and as she hugged him she raised her eyes to look at Anna.

Anna was smiling happily as she watched the two of them. 'Perfect,' she whispered to Demelza. 'You'll see, it will be perfect. But first you have to—'

'First I have to get down to the clinic,' Demelza said quickly. 'Irini is all on her own and—'

'Oh, Irini is a very capable girl! She got the top prize in the nursing school in Athens. The only reason she came back to the island is because she's betrothed to Demetrius who lives in the village. You don't need to worry about the clinic when Irini is in charge. She's clever enough to be a brain surgeon. I remember her first day at the village school. I said to her mother—'

'Did I hear you want a lift down to the resort, Demelza?' Giorgio interrupted as he came into the room.

Demelza smiled. 'Yes, please, Giorgio.' She stood up. 'Thank you so much for looking after Ianni, Anna. I've enjoyed talking to you and—'

'And you'll think about what I said and do something about it, won't you?' the older woman said, pulling herself to her feet so that she could give Demelza a hug.

Demelza gave her a wry smile. 'I'll have to think about it.'

Anna spread her arms wide. 'What is there to think about?'

'Leave the girl alone, Anna,' Giorgio said jovially. 'Whatever it is you're talking about, she'll make up her own mind. Come on, Demelza, let me get you down to the clinic.'

'Are you going to stay down at the resort with your mother, Ianni?' Giorgio said as he drove them down the winding road.

'Only during the day,' Ianni said quickly. 'I don't like staying there at night.'

'Why not?' Giorgio asked in a kindly voice.

Demelza noticed that Giorgio had reduced his speed to a leisurely pace. They were almost down at the resort and Giorgio obviously wanted to prolong the conversation.

The little boy screwed up his face as he thought of an answer. 'I'll tell you, Uncle Giorgio. And I can tell you, Demelza, but I know my daddy would be cross about it if I told him.'

'Cross about what, Ianni?' Giorgio asked.

He pulled the car to a halt at the far end of the car park and turned to smile encouragingly at his great-nephew.

All three of them were sitting on the front bench seat of the Jeep. Demelza reached across and put her hand over Ianni's. He clasped her fingers hard as he began to talk.

'Mum's got this awful boyfriend,' he said slowly.

'He swore at me. Told me to…well, go away. And when he stayed the night with Mum he…well, he sort of grunted, made funny noises I could hear through the wall, and I think he's horrid. But you mustn't tell Daddy, because he would go down and get cross with him and Mum would cry and it would be awful…just like it used to be when Mum and Dad were still married. A boyfriend came to see Mum one night when Dad was working at the hospital and then Dad came home and they all started shouting and…'

Ianni turned to Demelza as he began sobbing and she held him against her in a soothing embrace. When he'd stopped crying, she took out a tissue from her bag and gently wiped his face.

'What's the name of the boyfriend who comes to see your mum here at the resort, Ianni?' Giorgio asked, with steely calm.

Ianni pulled a face. 'Mum calls him Danny. He looks after the health club and the swimming pool during the day, but at night, when it's dark, he comes to see Mum. I think she likes him but I don't and I know he doesn't like me.'

Giorgio's face was as black as thunder as he climbed

down before reaching up to lift Ianni down on to the ground. As the little boy turned to walk away from the car, Giorgio whispered in Demelza's ear.

'Lydia's up to her old tricks again. She's man-mad. But the trouble is, she's looking for someone to support her and this Danny at the health club hasn't any money. Which is why she'd like to get back with Nick again. She doesn't stand a chance, Demelza. Can't think why she's still hanging around. This business of spending time with her son's all a pretence. If Nick did take her back, she'd soon show her true colours and stop the maternal bit once she was sure she'd hooked him.'

Demelza shivered. 'I'd better take him along to Lydia's. Thanks for the lift, Giorgio.'

'Be careful, Demelza. Lydia isn't to be trusted.'

'I know,' Demelza said. 'All I hope is that she's taking proper care of Ianni.'

'I'm going to have a word with Nick about that boy-friend of hers,' Giorgio said.

'But Ianni doesn't want him to know in case he creates a scene, as I'm sure he will.'

Giorgio shrugged. 'Someone has to tell him what Lydia's up to. The sooner she goes back to England and leaves Nick to get on with his own life, the better.'

Ianni was waiting for her at the edge of the car park. She said goodbye to Giorgio and hurried across to take the little boy by the hand. As they walked along to the beachfront suite occupied by Lydia, Ianni seemed to be dragging his feet on the sandy path.

'Do I have to spend the day with Mum?' he asked quietly.

'Mummy's looking forward to being with you,' Demelza said brightly, her heart going out to the little boy she loved so much. 'And you'll be coming home tonight.'

'And will you be there, Demelza?'

'Yes, I will,' Demelza said firmly. She'd come to a decision. It was all-or-nothing time now. She couldn't carry on, wondering what Lydia was up to. It was perfectly obvious now what her plans were. Giorgio was right. The sooner Lydia went back to England, the better!

She stopped walking outside Lydia's suite. All the curtains were closed. That was strange, in the middle of the morning—especially as she was expecting Ianni to arrive. Demelza went up to the door and knocked.

A bleary-eyed Lydia, holding a see-through chiffon robe around her, partially opened the door and peeped out.

'I've asked not to be disturbed except for room service... Oh, it's you, Demelza, and Ianni! But Anna phoned me earlier this morning to say Ianni was staying up in the village with her today. I'm not dressed, I haven't even—'

'Is that room service? About time!' A suntanned, muscular young man, wearing nothing but a pair of garishly coloured boxer shorts, appeared behind Lydia. 'Oh, it's the boy! I thought you said he wasn't coming today.'

'I didn't think he was,' Lydia said quickly.

Ianni was holding tightly to Demelza's hand as he tried to hide behind her. 'Don't leave me here, Demelza,' he whispered. 'That's the horrid man I told you about.'

'It's obvious you're busy today, Lydia,' Demelza said evenly, 'so I'll keep Ianni with me.'

She turned and quickly retraced her steps along the sandy path. Ianni was almost running now.

'Demelza, wait!' Lydia called after her in a horrified voice. 'I can explain!'

'I bet you can!' Demelza said, through gritted teeth.

'Can I really stay with you today, Demelza?' Ianni said, breaking into a full run to keep up with her. 'I can help you at the clinic. I'm going to be a doctor, you know, like Daddy. If you get a patient with a cut finger, I know how to put a plaster on. You just peel back the bits on the top till you get to the sticky bit and then you fold it round like this.'

Demelza squeezed his hand tightly. 'Of course you can stay with me, Ianni.'

They were already walking into the clinic and through to Demelza's consulting room. Going inside, she found Irini behind the curtains, leaning over a patient on the examination couch.

'Would you like to sit with Irini in Reception and draw me a picture, Ianni?' Demelza said quickly, giving him pencils and paper before he skipped back into the other room.

Behind the curtains, Irini filled her in on the details of the case before she went and sat with Ianni. The patient was a girl of nineteen called Selina who'd come out to Kopelos with her boyfriend and another couple. The other three had gone off to another island for the day. Selina had been going to go with them but she'd started to feel ill so had stayed behind.

Demelza became focussed on their patient as she leaned over her. Irini had told her that Selina was in a lot of abdominal pain.'

'Tell me exactly where it hurts most, Selina,' she

said, as she palpated the girl's abdomen, her experienced fingers working their way across the tense tissue.

Selina cried out in pain as Demelza's fingers pressed on the lower right side of her body.

'Sorry, Selina,' Demelza said gently. 'I just had to be sure where you were hurting. Just relax if you can. I'm going to give you something to ease the pain.'

She felt for the girl's pulse. It was rapid and faint. The reading on the chart also showed that her temperature was dangerously high.

'I want to take you to the hospital, Selina,' Demelza said. 'I'd like the doctor to see you, so I'm just going to give him a call.'

Demelza got through to Nick at the hospital fairly quickly and put him in the picture.

'I've got a nineteen-year-old girl with acute pain in the right iliac fossa, high temperature and rapid but faint pulse. It could be appendicitis or it could be an ectopic pregnancy. Either way, I'd like you to see her as soon as possible.'

'I'll phone Stavros and instruct him to bring you here while you prepare the patient,' Nick said quickly.

'Oh, and just one more thing, Nick. I've got Ianni with me. Lydia was…well, she didn't know he was coming today and she's…she's otherwise engaged.'

'But it was all arranged yesterday!'

'A mix-up. Anna had phoned to cancel the arrangement.'

'I can't think why she'd want to do that.'

Demelza knew exactly what Anna was up to! But there was no time to enlighten Nick now. 'Must go. See you in a few minutes.'

Ianni sat in the hospital reception, putting the finishing touches to the drawing he'd started at the clinic, whilst a couple of young nurses stayed close by to spoil him and give him anything he asked for.

In the small ante-theatre, Nick and Demelza leaned over their patient. Nick had decided to operate and Selina was now sedated.

From the answers she'd given to their questions, and taking into account all the clinical signs, it seemed likely that Selina was suffering from an ectopic pregnancy. She'd told them she hadn't had a period for two months. She was hoping she was pregnant because she and her boyfriend would like to have a baby.

Demelza looked down at her patient. It looked as if the baby that they'd hoped for had implanted itself in one of the two Fallopian tubes that led from the ovaries to the uterus. If the diagnosis was correct, the fertilised egg had implanted itself in the narrow tube. Now that it was growing bigger, it was dangerously close to bursting out through the wall of the tube.

A rupture of the Fallopian tube could be very dangerous. Demelza had seen a patient suffering from this in the past and she had nearly died from internal bleeding. So the sooner Nick operated the safer it would be.

Demelza had agreed to assist him. Having had the necessary experience, it seemed natural that she should want to be with her patient throughout the operation. The anaesthetist was preparing to administer the general anaesthetic. Now fully scrubbed and gowned, Demelza followed Nick into Theatre.

She looked across at him a short time later, under the bright lights as he located the minuscule embryo in the Fallopian tube. The tube had suffered from the trauma of being stretched to such a degree that it was now completely unviable.

'I'll have to excise the tube,' Nick said quietly. 'It can't be saved. But she still has a healthy tube on the other side which should be capable of functioning and delivering an egg into the uterus at a future date.'

Demelza nodded. 'It's never easy to explain all this to the patient afterwards.'

'I'd like you with me when we do that,' Nick said, his dark, expressive eyes above the mask looking straight at her.

'Of course,' she said.

Demelza gave Selina a few hours to recover fully from the effects of the anaesthetic before she broke the sad news that because the embryo had started growing in the wrong place it had been necessary to remove it, along with the damaged Fallopian tube, before it endangered her life.

Selina raised herself up from the pillows in the hospital bed and clung to Demelza as she cried softly.

'You've got another healthy Fallopian tube, Selina. When you feel strong enough, you can try for another baby,' Nick said, leaning over Demelza to comfort Selina.

'We hadn't intended to have a baby, me and Mark,' Selina said softly. 'But when I thought I might be pregnant, I got excited about it. And Mark wanted us to get married as soon as we got back from this holiday.'

'Mark's waiting outside,' Demelza said gently. 'Would you like to see him now?'

Selina gave a sad smile. 'Yes, please.'

Nick went outside to bring in a young man, who rushed over to Selina's bed and put his arms around her, holding her closely whilst he whispered comforting, soothing words.

Nick put his arm around Demelza's shoulders. 'Time for us to go.'

He turned to look at the night sister who'd just arrived for her turn of duty, and said something in rapid Greek.

'I've asked Sister to call me on my mobile if there are any problems,' Nick said, as he and Demelza walked out of the obstetrics ward.

Nick was carrying a sleeping Ianni in his arms. Before he'd gone into Theatre he'd suggested that Ianni might like to go to play with Lefteris at Katerina's house, but Ianni had been adamant that he wanted to stay at the hospital if that's where Demelza was working.

'I've never known Ianni to be as clingy as he was today,' Nick whispered, as he tucked up his little boy on the back seat of his car. 'Have you any idea what brought all this on?'

He settled himself in the front seat. Demelza fastened her seat belt beside him. She wanted very much to enlighten Nick, but Ianni had expressed his fear about how his father would react to the news that Lydia had another boyfriend.

'I'm not sure,' she said quietly, playing for time to consider the situation.

'Why are you being so secretive, Demelza?' Nick asked as he started up the engine and they moved forward into the darkness, away from the now silent hospital where only the muted nightlights shone out across the bay. 'You know something, don't you? I suspect it's something to do with Lydia and I've a pretty good idea what it might be. If it's affecting Ianni, please, tell me. I want to know everything that went on today before you came.'

'I'm trying to decide how much I should tell you.' She turned to look at Nick's stern profile as he turned the car into the deserted village street. 'I don't suppose Giorgio has been in touch with you today?'

'Demelza, I've been in hospital all day. Tell me what you know.'

Demelza shivered at the sound of Nick's harsh voice. She remembered how Ianni had told them about Nick's anger when he'd discovered Lydia's boyfriend.

'Let's get back and settle Ianni in his own bed first,' she said firmly.

CHAPTER TEN

DEMELZA tucked the cotton sheet around the sleeping Ianni as she settled him in his bed. He stirred as she kissed his cheek but didn't wake up.

'Ianni's fast asleep,' she said, as she went back into the living room.

Nick looked across at her. 'Come here and tell me what's been worrying him today.'

She deliberately settled herself on a chair at the other side of the small drinks table from Nick. She wanted to be able to watch his reaction to the news that his ex-wife, whom he may or may not have planned to remarry, was up to her old tricks again. She hoped he wouldn't raise his voice and waken Ianni.

'Would you like a glass of wine, Demelza?' Nick said, in a polite I-am-the-host voice.

'Later, perhaps.'

In spite of the warm temperature in the apartment, Demelza felt that the atmosphere was decidedly cool. She cleared her throat as she prepared to enlighten Nick.

'When I took Ianni down to see Lydia today, she had somebody with her.'

Nick frowned. 'Not the pool boy? Tall, about twenty, longish blond hair...?'

Demelza stared at him, perplexed. 'Did you know about Lydia's boyfriend?'

He gave a resigned sigh. 'Lydia's always had boy-friends. Danny is the man of the moment, so I'm told.

Trouble is, he's got no money so he won't be any use to Lydia.'

'That's what Giorgio said. He told me that Lydia is looking for a man who can keep her financially. He was planning to tell you what she was up to but—'

'Demelza, I understand my ex-wife perfectly! I was just putting on an act while she was here for Ianni's sake. I was being as polite and civil as I could. It was a big strain, I can tell you, but I knew that it was my duty to allow Ianni to get to know his mother again. When Lydia told me she wanted to come out here to see him, I thought it was only right that she should be able to make contact with her son again. I had hoped they might have got on better than they did, but I can see that nothing has changed. That's why I've given Lydia her marching orders.'

Demelza leaned forward. 'What do you mean?'

'I've given in her notice for the expensive apartment I was paying for. While there was a glimmer of hope of a successful mother-and-son relationship developing I was prepared to pay, but as soon as I found out that Lydia was seeing boyfriends again, I put a time limit on it. She goes back to England next week.'

'But when did you find out?'

'I've suspected this might be happening from the beginning when Ianni refused to sleep down there at Lydia's apartment after the first night. I didn't want to upset Ianni by asking him outright what the problem was but I had a pretty good idea. So I asked a couple of staff members to keep an eye on Lydia for me. They soon reported back about her toy boy, and that was when I was determined to make sure Ianni only went down to see his mother during the day. Lydia usually only entertains her boyfriends at night so I thought

Ianni would be perfectly safe. If I'd thought for one moment that Ianni was going to have to cope with—'

'Lydia was under the impression that Ianni wasn't coming down this morning,' Demelza interjected quickly, as she saw how angry Nick was becoming when he realised how Ianni had suffered. 'That's why Danny was still there.' She paused.

'Lydia came to see me soon after she arrived on the island,' she went on quietly. 'She tried to convince me that she'd been a dutiful wife and that it was your infidelity that broke up the marriage.'

Nick raised an eyebrow. 'She certainly can spin a good yarn! But anyone who knows Lydia will soon realise that she's a compulsive liar. I'm sorry she imposed herself on you and I wish I'd been there to shield you from her. I know how vitriolic she can be, and I could see, right from the start, that she regarded you as her rival.'

'But did you know she was trying to get you back?'

'Of course I did! Lydia is devious but utterly transparent! All that little-girl-help-me-down stuff she put on when she first arrived. It would have been amusing if it hadn't been so painfully obvious what she was up to. She's tried so many tricks to get me back but she must realise by now that I can't stand the sight of her. She wasn't fooled by me being polite when it mattered. She knew I was only doing it to keep the peace for Ianni's sake and it was wishful thinking on her part to think that I could possibly have any feelings for her.'

His eyes were troubled as he looked at Demelza. 'So it was Danny who upset Ianni, was it?'

'Ianni told me he didn't like Danny,' Demelza said evenly. 'He said he didn't want you to know about him because you would start shouting at Lydia and she would cry and—'

'Oh, my God, how Ianni has suffered because of me…' His voice choked with emotion.

Demelza leapt to her feet and went round the table to sit beside Nick, cradling him against her. 'Ianni's OK now that he's just with you. None of this was your fault, Nick.'

Nick raised his head. 'That's why I had to divorce Lydia. I felt nothing for her when I found out what she was really like. I thought it would be better for Ianni to live without all the anger and quarrelling that occurred because of Lydia's affairs.'

'Lydia told me that the two of you were hoping for a reconciliation. Every time you were with her I thought you might be getting back together. And for a while I…' She broke off as the awful memories came flooding back.

Nick drew her into his arms. 'I wish I'd been with you when Lydia invented the preposterous idea of a reconciliation! But if I *had* been there, she wouldn't have dared to spin her lies. The only woman I want in my life is you, Demelza. I want us to be together for ever and ever. I've been longing to ask you… Dare I hope that…? What I'm trying to say is…will you marry me?'

Demelza looked up at him, her heart beating so rapidly that she felt sure he could hear it. This was what she'd longed for but had hardly dared to hope would ever happen.

'Yes, I'll marry you,' she whispered, watching his expression change to sheer joy.

He kissed her gently on the lips with such tenderness that she felt her heart would burst with happiness.

'How do you think Ianni will react when we tell him?' she asked as she drew herself away.

Nick smiled. 'You must know he'll be over the moon! You've been so wonderful with him. You're the mother he should have had.'

'Don't say that,' she said quickly. 'I didn't try to replace his mother. I simply—'

'You can't be Ianni's birth mother, but you've already replaced Lydia in his affections.'

She looked up into Nick's eyes, so full of tenderness and love as the full realisation hit her that her dream was coming true. She wasn't going to think about all the problems of marrying someone who already had an ex-wife. She could cope with whatever came along if she held first place in Nick's heart.

He bent his head and kissed her once more. As his kiss deepened, he scooped her up into his arms and carried her through to his bedroom.

'You will stay with me tonight, won't you?' he whispered, as he laid her down on the cool cotton sheet. 'Now that we're engaged to be married, it doesn't matter if Ianni wanders in tomorrow morning.'

She smiled up at him, leaning forward to tug at the buttons of his shirt. 'Of course I'll stay. I'll stay for ever…'

The rosy glow from the morning sun pouring through the open window was trying to penetrate her eyelids. Slowly Demelza opened her eyes and looked at Nick lying beside her, his hair all rumpled, his mouth curved into a smile, as if he were reliving their passionate night.

She hadn't thought it possible to be so in love that you wanted to stay awake for the whole night. It had been blissful to turn over, try to sleep for a short while and then feel Nick's hands caressing her awake once more...turning to him, feeling the hardness of his insatiable body and being completely united with him in a wild, passionate embrace that climaxed in an ecstatic heaven far away from the real world.

Nick's phone was ringing. Demelza sighed. The real world was forcing itself upon them. They couldn't stay up on cloud nine entirely.

Nick groaned as he reached out, his fingers scrabbling around on the bedside table.

'Nick Capodistrias,' he mumbled. 'Ah, Giorgio.' He launched into rapid Greek which Demelza found impossible to follow. He was laughing as he put the phone down.

'My Uncle Giorgio sends his love and he's delighted with our news.'

'You told him already about...that we're going to be married?'

Said like that, she could barely believe it was happening—but it was. She'd agreed to marry the most wonderful man in the world and...

'Of course I told him. That's why he was ringing. To tell me to get rid of Lydia and marry you at the earliest opportunity. I told him it was all taken care of. So now he's off to tell Anna who will go round the village and invite everybody to the wedding.'

'But we haven't set a date yet, Nick.'

'The sooner the better. How about September?'

She took a deep breath. 'Make it October. It won't be quite so hot and I'll have time to get used to the idea that I'm going to be Mrs Nicholas Capodistrias. We'll also have to decide on a church and a place for a reception and—'

'All taken care of already. Giorgio and Anna think we should marry at the church above the harbour where my parents were married. And they will host the reception at Giorgio's taverna. And I warn you that Greek weddings can go on for days.'

'Don't you think we should go and waken Ianni and tell him what's happening?' Demelza said happily.

Nick gave her a rakish smile as he pulled her against him. 'Not yet… This is our time, before the family wakes up. We'll have to set our priorities for when we have more children, won't we? You do want our own babies, don't you, Demelza?'

She snuggled against him and gave herself up to the desire that was sweeping over her once more. 'Oh, yes. I want lots and lots and—'

'Better make a start now,' Nick whispered.

EPILOGUE

'I STILL can't believe we've been married for a whole year,' Demelza said, as she moved a couple of anniversary presents from the living-room table into the bedroom. 'Everybody has been so kind today at our lunch party, but I thought they'd never go!'

She flung herself down onto the bed and kicked off her shoes. 'These shoes are killing me. Far too posh for a wedding anniversary, but I thought I ought to look the part. Likewise this dress! Do you think we can duck out of the evening session at Giorgio's?'

Nick climbed on the bed beside her. 'Not a chance! Wedding anniversaries are nearly as prolonged as weddings. Remember how ours went on for the best part of a week?'

Demelza laughed as she began unbuttoning the low-cut silk bodice of the dress Katerina had designed and made for her. 'This dress is utterly exquisite but far too hot, even for October.'

'Let me do that for you, darling,' Nick said, leaning over her as he finished off the final silk-covered buttons.

Demelza smiled up at him. 'A dangerous move for me to start taking my clothes off if I've got to go out again.'

Nick gave her a wolfish grin. 'We've time for a short siesta. When is Katerina bringing the children back?'

'She begged to be allowed to keep the twins at her house for a couple of hours so that her own children can get to know them. And Ianni, of course, wouldn't let them out of his sight so he's gone, too.'

Nick leaned back against the pillows and put his arm around Demelza's shoulders. 'He's so proud of his little sisters.'

'I was pleased that he found Lucy and Anna interesting when they were born in June but he's delighted now they're four months and beginning to become real individuals. The best is yet to come.'

Nick sighed. 'You can say that again! My mother would be so proud her granddaughter's her namesake.'

'And Anna is over the moon every time she holds little Anna!'

Nick rolled onto one side. Poised on one elbow, he looked down at her with that tender expression that always melted her heart.

'So, all in all, we've made a good start on our family,' he said softly. 'When you've recovered from the twins we could have one or two more, couldn't we?'

Demelza smiled up at him. 'Oh, I'm sure that could be arranged, Doctor. In fact, I've made a start already.'

Nick's eyes widened. 'You mean… Demelza, what are you saying?'

'I did a pregnancy test this morning, but I wanted the twins to have pride of place today before we announce there's another baby on the way.'

He pulled her gently into his arms and kissed her lovingly on the lips. 'You're amazing!'

She smiled. 'I had some help, didn't I? I particularly remember that the twins' conception was fun. I think it was that evening last September when we went down to our deserted beach for a swim and afterwards… Good thing nobody was counting dates when we were married.'

Nick laughed. 'Oh, I think they probably were, but who cares?' He looked earnestly into her eyes. 'Do you still have the same medical theory about pregnancy and making love?'

She gave him a languid smile. 'You mean my tried and tested theory that if the mother is healthy, making love can be beneficial, Doctor?'

Nick ran his tantalising fingers over her skin. 'Exactly that, Sister!'

She snuggled against him. 'Why don't we find out…?'

Modern Romance™
...seduction and
passion guaranteed

Tender Romance™
...love affairs that
last a lifetime

Medical Romance™
...medical drama on
the pulse

Historical Romance™
...rich, vivid and
passionate

Sensual Romance™
...sassy, sexy and seductive

27 new titles every month.

*With all kinds of Romance for
every kind of mood...*

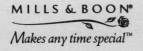

MILLS & BOON®

Makes any time special™

MAT4RS

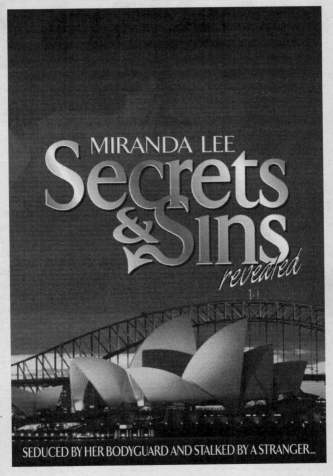

MIRANDA LEE

Secrets &Sins

revealed

SEDUCED BY HER BODYGUARD AND STALKED BY A STRANGER...

Available from 15th March 2002

*Available at most branches of WH Smith,
Tesco, Martins, Borders, Eason, Sainsbury's
and most good paperback bookshops.*

0402/35/MB34

2 FREE
books and a surprise gift!

We would like to take this opportunity to thank you for reading this Mills & Boon® book by offering you the chance to take TWO more specially selected titles from the Medical Romance™ series absolutely FREE! We're also making this offer to introduce you to the benefits of the Reader Service™—

- ★ FREE home delivery
- ★ FREE gifts and competitions
- ★ FREE monthly Newsletter
- ★ Exclusive Reader Service discount
- ★ Books available before they're in the shops

Accepting these FREE books and gift places you under no obligation to buy, you may cancel at any time, even after receiving your free shipment. Simply complete your details below and return the entire page to the address below. *You don't even need a stamp!*

YES! Please send me 2 free Medical Romance books and a surprise gift. I understand that unless you hear from me, I will receive 4 superb new titles every month for just £2.55 each, postage and packing free. I am under no obligation to purchase any books and may cancel my subscription at any time. The free books and gift will be mine to keep in any case.

M2ZEA

Ms/Mrs/Miss/Mr ....Initials......................................
BLOCK CAPITALS PLEASE

Surname ....

Address ....

....

....Postcode..............................

Send this whole page to:
UK: FREEPOST CN81, Croydon, CR9 3WZ
EIRE: PO Box 4546, Kilcock, County Kildare (stamp required)